STOLEN

STOLEN

A novel

Ed Dollinger

Full Court Press
Englewood Cliffs, New Jersey

First Edition

Copyright © 2013 by Edmund Dollinger

Published in the United States of America by Full Court Press, 601 Palisade Avenue Englewood Cliffs, NJ 07632 www.fullcourtpressnj.com

ISBN 978-1-938812-21-7
Library of Congress Control No. 2013947479

Editing and Book Design by Barry Sheinkopf for Bookshapers (www.bookshapers.com)

Colophon by Liz Sedlack
Cover art courtesy istockphoto.com

DEDICATION

A short while ago, a very bright, and perhaps brilliant, lady passed away. I had the privilege of being married to her for nearly fifty-three years. In her prime, Ruth was a true Renaissance woman. She could perform, with credible skill, nearly anything she wanted to do. Professionally, she was an actuary and a teacher. In addition she was an excellent linguist, a good musician, and a fine artist. Ruth donated her time and efforts to worthy causes, and to helping deserving people. She will be missed. This book is dedicated to her memory.

ACKNOWLEDGMENTS

I would like to thank my writing mentor, Barry Sheinkopf, for patiently teaching me how to turn a bunch of story ideas into a completed novel. Thanks, Barry—I couldn't have done it without you.

My thanks also to the excellent faculty, past and present, of New York University School of Law, for providing my hero, Ian Elkins, and his author, with an outstanding legal education .

CHAPTER 1

HERB KRONEN RUBBED HIS EYES. He'd been at it since right after lunch, when the accountants brought in the schedules. He looked up at the painting on the wall to the right of his desk and tried to laugh. It'd seemed funny when Jerry Sweeney hung it up eleven months before. That was the day they'd promoted Jerry to first assistant comptroller and given him an office with a window. On the same day Herb had been moved out of a cubicle, given Jerry's old interior private room, and made second assistant. It was a life-sized painting of a window. Jerry'd called it something to shoot for. If they all worked real hard there'd be another series of promotions up the line, and Herb would get Jerry's job and a real window.

"How's it going, buddy?" asked the near-seven-footer with the turned up nose and shock of curly red hair.

"My eyes," Herb replied, "are coming out of my head."

"What do you expect?" Jerry said. "It's third-quarter statement season. Put in some drops, and get a cup of coffee. It's going to be a long session. And remember," he concluded as he left, pointing to the picture.

Herb let out a breath as he reached into a side drawer of his gray-metal desk, extracted a bottle of eye drops, removed his rimless reading glasses, and headed for the men's room.

At eleven, they finally packed it in. They had proofed nearly ninety percent of the schedules and were too tired to complete the job accurately. It could be finished the next morning and be ready for the accountants by noon. As Herb trudged to his eight-year-old Pontiac in the middle of the employee's parking lot, he envied the comptroller and other officers of the company who parked next to the three-story industrial headquarters of his mid-cap corporate employer. Maybe Jerry was right. Maybe he *could* rise to the financial apex of the company. He did have an M.B.A. in accounting, though he was now only a bookkeeper with a title. There were times he regretted not having gone into public accounting, but this job paid better, and he needed the money.

He reached his Flushing home a little before midnight, lucky that traffic was light and he was able to find a metered spot two blocks from his building. Opening the door to his dark, cramped studio apartment depressed him. Good thing he was compulsively neat, or the place would be a real mess. He turned to the kitchen alcove and opened the fridge. The sandwich they'd ordered up for supper was wearing off, and he was starved. All he found was a half a loaf of rye bread and a few slices of luncheon meat. It would have to do. He had to be back in the office by eight to finish up; he didn't have time to go to the diner on Queens Boulevard.

"Barbara, could you get me some more coffee, *please?*" The near-eighty-year-old woman with heavily dyed chestnut hair held up her delicate china cup.

"Sure thing, Mom. I'll bring in the pot and fill us both up." Slim, dark-haired, Barbara left the dining room table, went to the spacious kitchen, and returned with a half-full carafe of coffee. She filled both cups and set the carafe down on a trivet on the side board.

The two women sipped in communal silence. After a while, the older woman spoke up. "It's good to have company."

"Good being with you too, Mom."

"It's very lonely without your father." Cora Kronen sniffed and blotted an eye.

Barbara groaned inwardly. Her mother was going into her maudlin routine. "I miss Dad, too."

Silence prevailed for another minute. The older woman's sad expression gradually turned into a sly smile. "I could go for another piece of the cake." She brushed crumbs from the front of a blue silk cocktail dress that had fit her better when she was less overweight. "In fact, why don't we both have one?"

"Not for me, Mother. Roger likes his women lean." Barbara cut a thin slice of glazed fruit cake and put it on her mother's plate.

"Can't you cut a bigger piece? I can afford it."

Barbara shook her head. "You know what the doctor said about your weight."

"Oh, what does he know?" Cora Kronen demanded. "I dieted when Burt was alive. Now, what other pleasures do I have?

Barbara Linden shook her head. "You have two loving children and three beautiful granddaughters. If you don't watch your diet, the diabetes is going to kill you before you can dance at any of the girls' weddings."

Cora smiled. "You're right, I do have you and the girls."

Barbara frowned. "And Herb. He visits you and takes you out most Sundays."

The old woman wrinkled her nose. "Yeah, in that rattle-trap old car. Can't he afford a newer one? He's got a job."

"Come on, Mom. He doesn't make that much. If you don't like his car, why don't you buy him a new one?"

She shook her head. "I will *not*! If he wants a new car, he can pay for it *himself*. I can't afford to pay for his extravagances. He'll get from me after I'm gone. If he behaves himself."

". . .You're very generous to me, Mother, and to the girls. Why can't you give him something? He works hard, and he's good to you."

Cora shook her head. "You don't understand, dear. When I was brought up, men took care of women. That's what his father believed, and so do I."

At four-thirty that afternoon, Barbara pulled her Lexus into the four-car garage of their Scarsdale home. Roger had beaten her home; his Hummer was parked in its usual spot. She shook her head as she wondered why an ordinary SUV wouldn't have done just as well. Probably the same reason he'd acquired the house. When you're a big corporate player, you have to keep up your image.

Inside, she followed the sounds of a T.V. newscast into their thirty-by-twenty-foot family room. Roger was seated on a love seat in front of the screen, his feet up on a matching white ottoman. His green golf pants and alligator shirt set off dark, wavy hair and an athletic build. On a stack table to his left lay an old-fashioned glass filled with ice and malt whiskey.

"I see the drinking lamp is lit," she said after pecking him on the lips. "Been home long?"

"About two sips' worth." He picked up the glass and took another.

She ambled to the bar, removed a bottle from the fridge, poured herself a white wine, and joined him. "Have a good game?"

"Quite. I nearly broke ninety."

"I'm impressed."

"So was the president."

"Are you the new executive V.P.?"

"Not yet, but I could be if the sales figures keep climbing."

"They will." She squeezed his hand.

"*Hey*, look at *that*," he said, pointing to the screen.

"Huh?"

"The company just moved up three slots on the Fortune 500."

"That's great. I'll bet it was all you in marketing."

"Tell that to Bill Nelson," he said, grinning. . . . "What's up for tonight?"

"Dinner at the club with the Ellises and the Grahams. I thought you kept a diary."

"Not for Saturday night. That's your domain."

"Yeah, woman's work, you chauvinist pig."

They both laughed.

"Seriously, I'd really like to get back to the work force."

He shook his head. "Not yet. The kids need you at home."

She bristled. "That's a lot of crap, and you know it."

He smiled sheepishly. "Yeah, but you know Bill Nelson."

"Who the hell does he think he is?"

"President of a company in which I want to make EVP." She groaned and took a sip of wine.

"Look, it's not so bad. Marcia Nelson's back teaching full time."

"But her kids are all in *college*, Rog, and Janie won't get there for another four years."

"What can I do? The Grahams are in the same boat. At least you've got Karen to commiserate with. . . . By the way, not to change the subject, how was your lunch with the old battle ax?"

She shrugged. "Not good. Mom's very difficult."

"No kidding." He rolled some scotch on his tongue. "I don't know how you put up with her. Those bi-weekly lunches must drive you nuts."

"It's not that bad. I can take it. The one I *really* feel for is Herb. He takes her out every week, and she does nothing but bitch about him."

He snickered. "That's nothing new. What's bothering her now?"

"She doesn't like his car. It's too small or old or something."

"Have him drive her in your father's car. It's practically a limo, and she loves it."

Barbara shook her head. "She sold the thing the year after he died. Didn't want to pay the insurance, and she hates to drive."

"Then why doesn't she buy *him* a new car? She can afford it."

"I suggested it to her, but she absolutely refused. Said

'men take care of women.'"

Roger shook his head slowly. "I feel sorry for the poor bastard. I guess she'll do well by him in her will."

"I hope so, but he could really use more money now. Isn't there any chance that—"

He held up his hand. "I wouldn't even dare suggest it. You know how Nelson feels about nepotism."

CHAPTER 2

W ILLIAM COHEN, III, WAS SEATED behind his twelve-
by-six-foot rectangular desk. A tall, slim man of
forty-five, he was dressed in what had become his
uniform, a three-piece blue-gray flannel suit from the Custom
Shop at Brooks Brothers. The desk had been his grandfather's,
one of the founders of Thatcher, Ryan, and Cohen, a prestigious firm of forty-three lawyers just under the fifty-person
limit that defined a small firm.

It was ten-thirty in the morning, and he was expecting a
visit from Cora Kronen, one of the clients his father, William,
Jr., had left to him, together with the leadership of the firm's
trusts and estates department. He grimaced as he contemplated how the meeting would probably begin. She would
kiss him, then ask how his daddy was, and, worst of all, call
him *Willie*.

His intercom buzzed. "Yes, Stella?"

"Mrs. Kronen is here."

"Show her into my office, and order a coffee service with

some butter cookies."

A few minutes later, Cora was escorted in, and the lawyer rose to greet her. She was wearing a brown silk suit from Ann Taylor which had been very attractive when she bought it before her husband's death but no longer fit her. He loathed fat women. "How are you, Mrs. Kronen?" he asked giving her the obligatory hug and double-cheek kiss.

"Please, Willie, it's Aunt Cora."

"Yes, Aunt Cora," he replied as he escorted her to a seat on the couch at the far end of his room. "I've ordered some coffee. It should be here shortly." He seated himself in an armchair on the opposite side of a glass-topped cocktail table.

A few minutes later, a uniformed maid brought in a tray with a vacuum carafe of coffee, a pitcher of cream, sweeteners, blue-flowered china cups and saucers, and a plate of cookies. They engaged in small talk while they sipped and Cora devoured eight of the cookies. "So—to what do I owe the pleasure of this visit?"

"Didn't your secretary tell you? I want to change my will."

The lawyer smiled. "Brenda did mention it to me. As a matter of fact, I have your file." He retrieved a slim folder and a yellow legal pad from his desk, resumed his seat and riffled through the pages of the will, pretending to read what he had carefully studied the hour before. "I see that you made twenty-five-thousand-dollar bequests to each of your three granddaughters and left the balance equally to your son and daughter."

She nodded.

"How much are you currently worth?"

She opened a large pocketbook, put on a pair of gold wire-framed glasses, and consulted a sheet of paper. "Including the house, a little over six million."

He scratched his thin, dark mustache. "What changes do you want to make?"

"I'd like to give one-third divided equally among my three granddaughters, Chelsey, Marci, and Janie."

"I thought the youngest was Jane."

"She is, but we call her Janie. She's so pretty. . . . They all are. Let me show you their pictures." She reached into her pocketbook and pulled out a small album.

The lawyer looked at the pictures and made the appropriate noises. After she returned the album, Cora added, "But they shouldn't get the money 'til they're twenty-five."

He thought for a moment. "We'll have to make a trust. Do you want them to get *anything* before twenty-five?"

"If they need it."

"I'll give the trustee discretion to pay income and principal to them. And the balance of the estate?"

"Sixty percent to my daughter, Barbara Linden, and forty percent to my son, Herbert Kronen."

The lawyer frowned.

"Something wrong?" she asked.

"I just wondered what your son's done that you're cutting him down."

She shrugged. "It's not that he's done *anything*, but my girls have always been much more loving. Why? Can't I do that?"

"Of course you can." The lawyer pondered for a moment. "I'll put in an interrorem clause."

"What's that?"

"Basically that, if he contests the will, he forfeits his bequest."

"Yes, definitely put that in."

Cohen skimmed the old will again. "I see that, in the present will, Herbert is the executor and I'm the first alternate. I guess you'll want to change that."

"Why should I?"

"I just thought that, since Barbara and her daughters get the lion's share of the estate, you might want her to be the executrix."

The old woman shook her head. "No, being an executor is men's work. Besides he's an accountant, so he'll know what to do."

"What about the trust for the granddaughters? Whom do you want as trustee?"

"How about my son-in-law, Roger, and you as the alternate?"

"Not a good idea. It'll cost him in taxes. I could be the trustee, if you want."

"No, I'd rather have a family member. Make Herbert the trustee, and you be the alternate."

"Are you sure?"

She nodded.

When Cora left, the lawyer shook his head and muttered, "Strange woman."

THAT SUNDAY WAS THE KIND of day the whole world looks forward to. The temperature was a comfortable 74, and, since it had rained the day before, the air was clear and sunny, the grass and flowers all sitting up and begging for approval. Herb Kronen pulled into Cora's driveway at 11:30; even his car, which had just come out of the shop, was running quietly.

He hoped his mother would be pleased.

"How's it going, Mom?" he asked when he found her in the dining room, drinking coffee and munching on sweet crackers.

"As well as can be expected," she replied with a sigh.

"What's the matter?" he asked, fearing another one of those days.

"It's nothing." She sniffed. "It's just been so lonely with your father gone."

He breathed a sigh of relief. This was the usual. He could deal with it. "I know. I miss him, too."

She blotted a tear. "I know you do. I shouldn't do this to you."

More of the same, he thought, stifling a chuckle. "It's okay, Mom, that's what sons are for."

She broke into a broad smile. "You're a good boy, Herbert. I couldn't have made it without you. Sit down." She rang a small brass bell. "I'll have Erna serve."

Luncheon was brought in by a scrawny, dark-haired woman in her mid-forties, dressed in a dark-green-and-white maid's costume. There was a platter loaded with smoked salmon, whitefish salad, egg salad, and sliced tomatoes, and another with cream cheese and assorted bagels. For dessert, she had Boston cream pie and coffee.

Herb was not a big eater, but while there was enough for five or six hungry people, nearly all of the food was consumed. It was no wonder that since his father's death, three years before, his mother had grown obese.

"Where would you like to go today?" he asked as she stuffed a third wedge of pie down her throat.

"You're the man. You decide," she replied with a sly

smile.

She's back in the groove, he mused. "How about the Neuberger Museum in Purchase? You haven't been there in a while. Maybe they have a new exhibit."

"Too far." She frowned. "Your car makes too much noise. I'll get a headache."

He smiled. She's playing the same old game. "The car's fine, Mom. I just took it out of the shop. It's running quiet as a whisper."

She pondered. "No, still too far. How about the Cloisters? I haven't seen the tapestries for quite a while."

"Whatever you say, Mom."

HERB GOT HOME AT SEVEN-THIRTY. The visit to the museum had gone just fine; his mother had seemed quite happy. He'd offered to take her out to dinner, but she'd preferred eating at home and hadn't invited him to join her. He'd left her at the house at about five and gone to dinner in a local Queens restaurant.

As he entered his apartment, he was feeling quite mellow. He noticed that the answering machine was flickering. The call was from his sister. He returned it immediately.

"Hi, Roger. How's it going?"

"Where the hell have you *been*? Barbara's *frantic*."

"What's the matter?"

"Your mother is in the hospital. She's had a heart attack."

CHAPTER 3

AT ONE O'CLOCK ON A TUESDAY in early October, Ian Elkins and his boss, Mark Rooney, were having lunch at Rooney's over-sized desk. The room was the only three-windowed office in the law office suite on the ground floor of an apartment house just three blocks from the Bronx County Courthouse. Ian was working on a chef's salad while his boss wolfed down a foot-long meatball hero. Rooney was a generous man and frequently bought his young associate lunch so that they could discuss cases while they ate.

"Watch it," Ian warned. "The gravy's just about to drip on your tie."

"Thanks, kid," Rooney replied holding the sandwich over his plate and leaning for his next bite. "Kathy'd kill me if I ruined this one. She bought it for me last Christmas."

Half an hour later, the two had gone through lunch and three of Ian's cases when the intercom buzzed. "Yes, Rosie?" Rooney listened for a moment, pressed the hold button and passed the receiver to Ian. "It's for you. A Mr. Cowen."

"Hello, Mr. Cowen. . . ? Oh, it's you, Bill. I guess the receptionist got the name wrong. . . . I'm in with my boss now. Can I call you back in about ten minutes?" Ian scribbled a number on a pad and hung up.

"What's that about?" Rooney asked.

"It's Bill Cohen. He's the estates partner at Thatcher, Ryan. I had a number of things with him when I was with the court. He has a Bronx estate matter he wants to refer to me."

"New business? Great. Don't let *me* keep you."

Later that afternoon, Ian was poring over a file in his minuscule interior office when he looked up to see Rooney hovering over his cluttered desk. "So?" the big man asked.

"Huh?"

"The new case. What's it about?"

"Oh." Ian smiled. "Bill drew a will for an old lady who lived in Riverdale. She left everything to her son, her daughter, and her daughter's kids. The will gave the son the short end of the estate *and* made him the executor and the trustee of his sister's daughters's trusts."

Rooney scratched his second chin. "That was dumb. How come he's referring the estate to you? He's a hot-shot estates lawyer, isn't he?"

Ian shook his head. "It's not the estate he's referring."

Rooney gave him a puzzled look.

"Bill got the estate originally and probated the will. Then, a few months later, the son took it away from him and gave it to a Queens lawyer. He told Bill he wanted a lawyer with an office near where he lived."

"Then what's he referring to us?"

"The daughter came in to see him. She said she thought her brother was playing fast and loose with the estate and the trusts."

Rooney nodded. "And since he'd been representing the brother, Cohen has a conflict of interest and can't represent the sister."

"Exactly. He told me to expect a call from the daughter." Ian pushed aside the file he was working on and looked down at a yellow legal pad. "Barbara Linden."

THAT EVENING IN SCARSDALE, BARBARA and Roger Linden, and their youngest daughter, Janie, were gathered at a round table in their kitchen dining alcove. The table, which could comfortably seat six, had been chosen to allow the entire Linden family to dine informally together, but with two of their daughters away at college, it looked somewhat bare. "May I be excused?" asked Janie, pushing aside a half-eaten slice of apple pie. "I have a lot of homework to do."

"Of course, dear," Barbara replied.

"Aren't you going to finish your pie and milk?" asked Roger.

"Please, Daddy, I'm full. . . . I guess you could ship it to the poor starving children in Asia," she concluded disentangling her blonde ponytail from the chair.

Roger started to laugh but caught himself. "Seriously, Janie, you don't eat enough. It's not healthy."

Barbara held up her hand. "Leave it be, Rog. She eats enough, and you know girls want to maintain their knockout figures."

He threw up his hands up in mock surrender.

When Janie left, Barbara refilled their coffee cups and sat down. "How'd it go today?"

"Pretty good. You? "You see the lawyer?"

She nodded. "I was there today."

"What'd he say?"

"That he had a conflict of interest, because he'd represented Herb before."

Roger knitted his brow.

"He referred me to another lawyer. A man named Elkins. Said he's very good. Used to work in the surrogate's court."

"You make an appointment with this Elkins?"

"Not yet. Mr. Cohen will be calling him and told me to wait a day or two."

"Good Give me his name. I'll have our company's counsel check him out."

Barbara sipped her coffee and frowned. ". . . Rog?"

"Yes, dear?"

"I don't know."

"Don't know what?"

She hesitated. "If I should be doing this. He's my *brother*."

Roger Linden shook his head. "Barbara, I understand your reticence, but you're talking about a lot of money, and a good deal of it belongs to the girls."

"But Mom treated him so badly. Maybe we should let him recoup some of it."

Roger tightened his jaw. "Look, Barbara, I don't begrudge him anything. If he has a problem, let him ask for help, and I'll consider it sympathetically. But what he's doing is wrong. If Herb's been *stealing*, we've got to stop him."

CHAPTER 4

BY MID-OCTOBER MOST OF THE leaves had fallen. On the third Friday of the month, Ian Elkins pulled his ancient Volvo onto his in-laws' driveway. "I see your dad got all the leaves up. He's not doing it *himself* anymore, is he?"

"I sure hope not," his wife Helen replied. "I remember him doing it when I was growing up, before he unloaded the job on *me*."

"We see Grandma and Grandpa?" asked three-year-old Carol.

"You bet, sweetie. What do you think Grandma made for dinner?"

The little girl giggled. "That's easy, Daddy. Grandma always makes chicken."

"Who else are we going to see?" asked Helen.

The little girl knit her brow.

"Whom do we see when we visit Grandma and Grandpa? . . . Aunt . . . ?"

Carol's face brightened. "Aunt *Betty*."

"And?" Helen added.

"Uncle Eric."

Helen smiled. "And who else? . . . Cousin . . .?"

"No like Cousin Freddie."

"Why not?" asked Ian.

"Won't *play* with me. I'm too *little*."

Helen hugged her daughter. "We'll have to talk to him about that."

"It's okay, Mommy. I play with Grandpa. He's a funny man."

"Who's a funny man?" boomed a nearly fat man with thinning gray hair, as the door to the five-bedroom colonial opened and, he came down the three railed steps onto the walk and scooped his granddaughter into his arms.

"*You* are, Grandpa," she declared, burying her head just above his bulging stomach.

"And you're a funny monkey, too," he replied. He kissed her and ran his hand down the back of her head. "So is anybody coming in, or do you want to miss Grandma's roast chicken with sweet potatoes, and apple pie with ice cream?"

"Coming, Dad," replied Helen, as Sam Kaplan carried the child into the house.

"Are they here?" asked Molly Kaplan. "I was getting lonely."

"What about Betty and Eric?" asked Ian. His brother-in-law was a partner in Sam's accounting practice.

"Freddie's got a bad cold, so they couldn't make it."

"Poor Freddie," declared Helen. "I guess you've got Grandpa all to yourself." She kissed Carol.

"Who's making the drinks?" Sam asked. Carol giggled as he tickled her. "I've got something better to do than be a bartender."

"I'll do it, Dad," replied Ian. "You having the usual?"

"When have you seen me drink anything but a martini before dinner?"

"Where's the wine?"

"Chilling on the dining room table."

As Ian went to the bar, he considered the family he'd married into. Sam was more than just an accountant. He was a modern-day Solomon, an eager giver of world-class advice and willing sounding board for other people's problems. Molly was the very prototype of a Jewish mother and willing substitute for his own, who was in a nursing home, wasting away in the late stages of Alzheimer's. Molly was a great cook, especially of chicken, which she made for every Friday night's dinner—a command performance for the entire immediate family. Helen's older sister, Betty, was sweet although not nearly as smart, Eric, a pain in the ass with a penchant for making hurtful comments. Helen's older brother, a physician, lived in Chicago. He and his family seemed nice, but Ian didn't know them very well.

"Where's my drink?" asked Sam.

"Coming, Dad," Ian replied. He dropped ice into a glass cocktail shaker, added precisely three drops of extra-dry imported vermouth, five ounces of Tanqueray gin, and stirred. Sam believed a martini should never be shaken, that it bruised the gin. Pouring the first drink from the shaker, Ian added a lemon peel, made himself a Red Label on the rocks, and carried the drinks on a small tray into the dining room, where he poured two white wines for the women. When he got to the living room, Molly and Helen were seated on the couch, Sam on an easy chair with Carol on his lap, playing Patty Cake.

"Where's *my* cocktail, Daddy?" the little girl demanded.

"One Coke cocktail coming up."

"Ian," Sam asked, "what's exciting in the law lately?"

As Ian was about to begin, a voice emerged from the kitchen. "All ready, Mrs. K."

Molly Kaplan raised her statuesque torso from the couch, brushed back a few strands of her brown-dyed hair, and announced, "Dinner is on the table. Everybody come in *now*. Legal excitement will have to keep until we finish dessert."

They fell upon fresh fruit cups, green salad, roast chicken with rosemary and thyme, accompanied by carrots and sweet potatoes, followed by warm apple pie topped with vanilla ice cream. When they retired to the living room for coffee, Sam turned to his wife. "Can we have some legal excitement now?"

She nodded to Ian.

"I hope I won't disappoint you," he began. "A woman came in to see me about her mother's estate."

"A big one, I hope?" Molly interjected.

"A few million, but we won't be representing the estate."

Sam's expression grew puzzled .

"Her brother's the executor, and he took the estate away from the lawyer who drew the will, and who referred the matter to me. She thinks her brother's been stealing from the estate."

Molly shook her head vigorously. "That's terrible, stealing from your mother."

"It's not really stealing from his mother. She's dead. He's really taking it from his sister and her three children," Ian replied.

"*Oy.* You lawyers are so technical," Molly declared. "But

I love you just the same."

Sam chuckled. "What makes her think he's stealing?"

"Her mother told her that she was worth about six million, including the house. Her will provided that one-third goes to her three granddaughters in trust, the balance split sixty percent to her and forty percent to the brother."

Sam pursed his lips. "Looks like he got the short end of the stick. . . . Yet she made *him* the executor?"

"*And* trustee, with no commissions from either the estate or the trusts."

"I can see why he would steal," said Sam. "How'd he do it?"

"That's the interesting part. He's an accountant, and he's either very smart or very stupid. After the old lady had her heart attack, he ran her affairs under a power of attorney. When she died, it turned out that most of her bank accounts and securities were in joint names with the son. He told her sister that their mother felt badly about how she'd treated him, especially since he was caring for her after the heart attack, and that she'd made up for it with the joint accounts. According to what he told her, out of the six-million-dollar estate he got two and a half million in joint accounts. The granddaughters split a little over three-quarters of a million, and he gets forty percent of the balance."

Sam shook his head. "Daughter must be madder than hell. Probably wants to string him up."

"That's the funny part. She doesn't really want to do anything to him. Feels sorry for him and the way her mother treated him. Her husband had to put on a lot of pressure to make her come to see me."

"Sounds like a tough case. You need any accounting help

don't hesitate."

"Only if you let the client pay you."

THE PHONE RANG IN A ONE-WINDOWED office in another part of town. "Kronen."

"How come the first assistant comptroller of a major corporation is picking up his own telephone?"

Herb half-chuckled and half-groaned. Sally had been pulling the same routine ever since they started going together. "Because his secretary went home at five." He looked at the window that had, in fact, recently replaced the painting of one in his old office, which he had passed on to his successor in the second-assistant spot. If Jerry ever became C.F.O., maybe he'd get two more windows. Facing forward he admired the Picasso reproduction and the Sheinkopf photo of a waterfall he'd acquired at a charity art auction.

"And how come," she asked, "the first assistant comptroller of a major public corporation is still working at six-thirty on a Friday evening, when his secretary went home at five?"

"Because she gets paid overtime for working past five, and he doesn't. Besides, it's only six-twenty. What're you, taking a survey?"

"Seems that way," she replied. "When's the workaholic prince coming to pick up his princess?"

"Unless Jerry dumps another emergency on me, I should be done in half an hour. I'll pick you up at eight."

"Make it 7:30, and you'd better be ready to feed me well. I'm starving."

"Not as much as I'm starving for you," he quipped as he put down the phone.

At seven forty-five, Herb pulled his ancient Pontiac into

the driveway of a twenty-five-story co-op on Queens Boulevard about a mile from his apartment. "Can I help you, sir?" asked the uniformed doorman, poking his head through the window of Herb's car.

"Yes, Larry, would you please call Ms. Martinis in seventeen-o-seven?"

"Oh, it's you, Mr. Kronen. I'll call up."

The doorman returned a minute later. "Ms. Martinis said she'd be down in a few minutes. Whyn't you pull over to the waiting area?"

Fifteen minutes later a tall, willowy blonde in a long navy coat with a white fur collar flounced out of the building and sidled up. Herb got out of his car and held open the door for her. After she was seated, they embraced and kissed deeply. He could taste the remnants of a Manhattan on her active tongue.

"Where do you want to eat?" he asked. "How about Primavera?"

"You won't get away that cheap." She lit a cigarette with a silver lighter.

"I don't know where else we can go without reservations." He wished she didn't smoke. It was one of the few things that bothered him about her, although it was kind of cool when she lit up after sex.

"It's a good thing you have me to make plans. We have a nine o'clock reservation at Le Jardin, so step on it."

Traffic was light, and they made it from Queens, New York, to Fort Lee, New Jersey, in under an hour. As he surrendered the car to the attendant, she whispered into his ear, 'Isn't it time you traded up to a Mercedes?"

"You sound like my mother."

She chuckled. "See, she wasn't all wrong, and you can use her money to prove it."

They were soon seated at one of the inner tables overlooking the Hudson River. "How'd you get one of the good tables at the last minute?" he asked after the waiter took their drink order.

She smiled. "That's my secret."

"Bet I can guess."

She smiled and spread her palms.

The waiter returned with drinks and menus, recited the specials, and left when they waved him off.

Herb toyed with his cabernet. "I'll bet this is one of your company's watering holes for visiting firemen."

"Could be." She took a long pull on her perfect bourbon Manhattan.

He laughed. "What other secrets will you reveal?"

"I've revealed one already."

He knit his brow.

"Remember what I said about your old clunker? You'd make a *much* better impression driving a new Mercedes."

"Hey, I'm only salaried middle management. How can I afford it?"

"I told you. Let Cora buy it for you."

"What if I have to give it back?"

"You won't. Just keep listening to me."

CHAPTER 5

HARLEY GOLDBERG SHARED A SUITE of offices in Long Island City with five other lawyers. Actually, "shared" is too strong a word. He rented the smallest room in the suite from Jack O'Brien, who ran a personal-injury and workers-comp mill. When Harley was looking for space to set up for himself after leaving the small firm he worked for after graduating from Brooklyn Law, he'd been introduced to O'Brien, who had a spare room in his suite. The jowly red-faced man had laughed when he heard the name. "How the hell did a Goldberg get called Harley?"

Used to jibes like that, the other had replied, "From my mother. She was born a Davidson."

"Then why didn't you go into the motorcycle business?"

"They wouldn't let me in."

"How come?"

"My great-grandfather wasn't smart enough to buy into the family business. He couldn't imagine anybody buying a motorcycle."

O'Brien had laughed. "You're full of shit, but I like you." And he had. They'd made a deal: Harley would give all of his negligence and comp to Jack, who farmed all his unrelated business in the reverse direction. One of the better pieces of business had been the six-million-dollar estate Harley'd gotten through a recommendation from Jack's nephew, Jerry Sweeney.

Harley was seated behind his desk in his two-windowed twelve-by-fifteen room when the intercom buzzed. "Yes, Kathleen."

"Mr. Kronen is on the line."

". . .Afternoon, Herb. How're you doing?"

"Okay, I guess."

"*Guess?*"

"I got a problem."

"That's what you have me for. What is it?"

"I got a letter from a lawyer."

"He trying to steal you from me?" Harley replied with a laugh, scratching his blond mustache.

"Funny man."

"I've got to be. I'm the only non-Irishman in the office. What the guy want?"

"He represents my sister. Says she wants an accounting."

"Fax it to me. "

A HALF HOUR LATER THE LAWYER got another call from his client. "Yes, Herb."

"Did you get it?"

"Of course I did."

"What do you think?"

"That your sister wants an accounting."

"So what should we *do*?" Herb's voice was breathy.

"Give it to her," the lawyer replied with a snicker. "Plug together some schedules. . . . But send them to me."

"What about the joint accounts?"

"What about them? Don't show *them*. They're not part of the probate estate."

"Won't she complain? She knows about them."

"If she does, we'll deal with it."

"How?"

"Come on, Herb.. . .we've been over this loads of times. Sally gave you good advice. The paperwork is solid."

"What if my sister sues?"

"I thought she loved you."

"Yeah, but my brother-in-law is pushing her."

"So? . . . Look, Herb, if they push too hard we can always settle. That's what you expected to do anyway."

WHEN IAN RETURNED FROM LANDLORD and tenant court the next day, he noticed his boss, Mark Rooney, lounging in the hallway off the reception area. He was about to head to his room when the big man motioned him over. What's up, Mark?" Ian asked after seating himself opposite the middle of Rooney's three windows.

"I want you to do something for me, kid."

"Sure thing, boss," he replied with a smile. "What is it?"

Rooney frowned. "I hate to stick you with this, but I don't know who else I can trust." He picked up the gold cup with *Boss* emblazoned on it, took a sip, and spit it back. The coffee was cold.

"You've got a whole bunch of good guys in the office."

"True," Rooney allowed, "but you have one thing that

they don't—an overdeveloped conscience."

"I thought that was one of my problems."

Rooney grinned. "Usually it is. We'd all be better off if you were a little more practical. . . . But not in this case. . . . You know Kathy's kid brother?"

"That's Barney?"

Rooney nodded.

"Yeah, I met him at a couple of the Christmas parties. Isn't he the black sheep of the family?"

"You could say that," Rooney replied with a chuckle. "But that's the *nicest* thing I ever heard said about him . . . . Look—the son of a bitch is in serious trouble. There's an indictment out against him for criminal usury in the first degree."

Ian grimaced. "That is *serious*." He looked out the window behind Rooney, noticing the clotheslines in the back of the apartment building. He knew that the windows facing the Grand Concourse had been bricked up for security purposes, and wondered why they'd bothered leaving the crappy view.

"Yeah. He could get fifteen years. Kathy wants me to represent him."

"Couldn't do better."

"Thanks, but I don't want to touch it. I want *you* to."

Ian's expression changed. "Why? I should be the last choice. I haven't done any criminal. Kevin and Mike take what you can't handle."

Rooney exhaled. "I can't trust either of them for this one. Barney was running an unlicensed small loan office. He was making loans at two and a quarter percent a month. That comes to twenty-seven percent. Some detectives ran a sting and borrowed five thou from him, and at the end of the month him paid back $5,125.00. When he took the money, they slapped the cuffs on him." Rooney passed him a copy of the penal code open to *Criminal Usury*.

After reading the sections, Ian was puzzled. "Why first degree? It's *second*, unless he has a prior or it's part of a scheme or business."

"They're claiming he was *in* the usury business. Barney claims he only did it this one time 'to help out a friend.' Says he went to grade school with the guy. He also says that he was only supposed to get $5,100.00, but the guy slipped in an additional twenty-five."

"Maybe he's telling the truth, and he has a defense."

Rooney shook his head. "My brother-in-law is a lying son of a bitch. I wouldn't be talking to you if Kathy hadn't pressed me. If *I* handle it, he's going to want to testify and tell his lies, and he'll try to get Kathy to push me into suborning perjury. If I give it to Kevin or Mike, they'll be tempted to cut corners because he's my brother-in-law."

"Then why me?"

"Kathy knows you have high moral principles and won't go along with those kinds of shenanigans. We'll all help you with the case, but *you've* got the job of keeping my brother-in-law in line so none of us lose our licenses."

CHAPTER 6

OPPOSITES, IT IS SAID, ATTRACT, but in the case of the marriage between Mark Rooney and Kathleen Moran, the application of that truism was somewhat strained. They had first met at a post-football game party on the Rosehill campus of Fordham University. Fordham had just beaten N.Y.U. in its only victory of the season. He was a senior, a reserve offensive tackle who had been put in for one down series after the victory was iced; she was a freshman cheerleader. He was over six feet tall with a tendency to over-weight, she five feet two and near rail-thin petite. Mark was a pre-law with fair grades, brash and outgoing, and a success-ful campus politician. Kathy, quiet, a music major with a fine alto voice and considerable skills on the piano, was running straight A's. At the party he'd impressed her as a boor. He'd considered her a pretty but snobbish, an ice maiden.

Their paths didn't cross again until three years later, when they met at a dinner hosted by her uncle, Howard McCann, a professor at the law school and faculty advisor to the law review, for which Mark was the business editor. At the dinner the young man, awed by being in his professor's home, had been on his best behavior and considerably subdued. Kathy, though hardly enchanted by him, did enjoy his company and was more than polite. A few days later, Kathy's mother had had told her that Uncle Howard thought the young man had good prospects, and when Mark called the next week she'd accepted a date.

They got along quite well and dated steadily, though for Kathy sex before marriage was out of the question. This reticence had probably stood her in good stead; they'd married shortly after Mark passed the bar. True to McCann's predictions and with his assistance, the young man had gone to work at the mid-sized firm to which the professor was of counsel. Several years later, Rooney and his wife's uncle had formed the Bronx law firm of McCann and Rooney, which in time became Mark Rooney and Associates when the professor was elected Bronx County Surrogate.

The marriage, though childless, was quite happy, and while her husband's girth had increased considerably over the years, Kathy'd remained slender. One might have thought that, when a man outweighed his wife nearly three-to-one, he would be the dominant force in the marriage, but Rooney both adored and feared his spouse, and she unquestionably ruled the roost. Most of the time she was sweet and caring. When angered, her cold, quiet fury made him cringe. Fortunately, she rarely interfered in his law practice—though when her favorite younger brother, Barney, was threatened, Kathy became a lioness.

THE DAY AFTER ROONEY DRAFTED Ian as Barney's counsel, Kathy dropped by the office unannounced. A few minutes later Ian's intercom buzzed. "Yes, Rosie?"

"Mr. Rooney wants you in his office *now*."

Upon mounting the bridge, Ian found the captain and his mate drinking coffee. He pecked Kathy on the cheek and seated himself in front of the third cup on the big man's desk.

For the next few minutes the only sounds in the room involved the consumption of coffee. Then Mark broke the near silence. "Kathy thought you would be better able to represent Barney if you knew something about him."

"That sounds like a good idea," Ian replied.

"We're going out to lunch now, and I'll have Kathy join you in the library at about two. . . . I'd invite you along, but we have some family business to discuss."

"I look forward to it," Ian replied. "Enjoy your lunch." As he returned to his office, he wished Helen could have attended the meeting, too.

AS A LAWYER, HARLEY GOLDBERG'S BEST and worst qualities were substantially similar. He had an irrepressible driving force that frequently bowled over the opposition, but it was coupled with the tendency to shoot from the hip. He was aware of the deficiency and generally made a conscious effort to hold himself in check until he had analyzed the situation and mentally counted to ten, but when vexed, his control sometimes slipped and he would lash out, frequently with sarcasm. Returning from court that afternoon, he was in a foul mood. He thought he'd been abused by both the judge and his client, and he was seeking vengeance.

As he came through the office door, the aging but still attractive receptionist smoothed back her long red hair and handed the lawyer three message slips.

"Kathleen—they're all from the same person."

"I know, Mr. Goldberg." She shook her head. "He's most insistent. He's been calling every hour. At noon he accused me of hiding you."

"I'll call him back."

The phone rang, and the receptionist picked up. A moment later, she pressed the hold button. "You won't have to. He's on the line now."

Harley went to his office and picked up the phone. "This is Harley Goldberg. How may I help you?"

"Who the hell do you think you are?"

The lawyer tightened his jaw. "I believe I just told you. You're Mr. Linden, I assume?"

"Yes. Roger Linden, executive vice-president of Universal Electronics."

A smile crossed Harley's face. "A very good company. Are you selling me stock, or are you folks looking for a lawyer?"

"Very funny," Linden growled.

"Then why did you call me?"

"The Kronen estate."

"What about it?"

"Your client is stealing money from my wife and daughters."

"Really? . . . Have your wife and daughters authorized this call?"

"*What?*" Linden shouted. "What the hell does *that* mean?"

"I just wanted to find out whether to sue your wife and daughters for slander, or just you. . . . More to the point, Mr. Linden, this is none of your business. If your wife or daughters have a problem, let them talk to their lawyer." Harley hung up.

"WHAT'S BOTHERING YOU, DARLING?" Helen asked as she and Ian left the dinner bar and headed into the living room for coffee and TV. "Are you feeling alright?"

"Physically, yes."

"But?"

"Damn case is driving me up a wall."

She snickered. "How unusual."

His face reddened. "I'm sorry. I'm always doing this to you. I guess I don't have the temperament to be a lawyer. Everything seems to bother me."

She smiled. "That's not so bad. It shows you care. Tell me about it."

"It's the usury business."

"Usury?" She knit her brow. "Criminal?"

He nodded.

"I didn't think you did criminal cases."

"I don't. This is Kathy's brother, and Mark thinks he's as guilty as sin. He's using me because he thinks I'm the only one in the office who won't let the client suborn perjury."

She chuckled. "I'm married to the office saint."

He blushed even more. "I guess so."

"What happened today?"

"Kathy came into the office, and Mark told me to meet with her so she could tell me about her brother."

"And?"

"And! She spent half an hour lecturing me about what a nice, charming person Barney was, and that I was not to take a plea, not let him be convicted, and most of all keep him out of jail."

She shook her head. "You poor baby. Mark wants a saint, and Kathy wants a miracle worker." She hugged him.

CHAPTER 7

A BRIGHT SUNNY AFTERNOON: IAN longed to be pushing his daughter in a swing at the local playground, but...it was Thursday and he was at his desk, reading over the files for his Friday landlord-and-tenant cases. His concentration broke when the intercom buzzed.

"Mr. Barney Moran is here to see you," Rosie told him.

"...His appointment isn't until tomorrow."

"He said something came up and he had to change it. He's *sure* you'll see him now."

"I have ten cases on the Landlord and Tenant calendar, three of which may go to trial. . . . Oh, well, show him into the library."

As Ian approached the room at the center of Rooney's hive, he noticed a strong odor of tobacco. What the hell, he thought, this is supposed to be a non-smoking office. His client was seated at the table, puffing on a sizeable cigar. "Hello, Ian, me boy," said the florid-faced fellow with the black handlebar mustache in a thick Irish brogue. As he turned to shake hands an ash fell on the table. "Sorry, I didn't see a receptacle."

"That's because it's a no-smoking office." Ian shook his hand then said into the intercom, "Rosie, would you please find me an ashtray?"

"Well, you said you wanted to talk about me case, so here I am."

Ian clenched his teeth but decided not to get into a war over the date. He reached into his file, pulled out the copy of the indictment, and spread it out on the table. "They're charging you with making the loan 'as part of a scheme or business of making or collecting usurious loans.'"

Barney read the lines Ian had pointed to. "So?"

"So, other than the $5,000.00 you lent Detective Mullins, have you made any other loans?"

The man knit his brow. "I might have. Why, haven't you ever loaned anyone some money?"

Ian gritted his teeth. "Come on, Barney, you know what this is about. If you only made one loan, the one to Mullins, they'd have charged you with second degree, which is a Class E Felony with a four year max. How many loans have you *made* in the last month?"

The man smiled sheepishly. "Ian, I'm not a big-timer. I make an occasional loan to help out a friend—like I thought Timmy Mullins was."

"How many friends did you help out with a loan *last month*?"

Barney knit his brow and seemed to fall deep in thought. "Maybe a few."

Ian exhaled strongly. "How many?"

"How should I know?" He shook his head. "Besides,

why d'you want to know?"

"So I can know almost as much about the case as the DA."

"What could *he* know?"

"Look, Barney," Ian replied, pointing at another line on the page. "They're also charging you with possession of usurious loan records. "When your *friend* Timmy arrested you, I assume he searched your office and took your files."

"Then you'd better ask him."

Ian switched tack. "What do you do for a living?"

Moran smiled. "A little of this, a little of that."

ON FRIDAY AFTER COURT, IAN WAS seated in Rooney's office, as usual lunching at his desk. "How'd you make out today?" the big man asked between bites of a tuna hero.

"It went okay. I won one, settled two on trial, and worked out the rest."

Rooney let out a breath. "Glad to hear it. I was a little worried when my damned brother-in-law ruined your prep."

Ian nodded. "I was able to prepare when he left, but Helen was miffed I didn't get home 'til eight."

"I assume you told her that the law's a jealous mistress."

"That doesn't work any more, boss."

Rooney chuckled. "Hasn't worked with Kathy for years." He downed some coffee. "How'd it go with my brother-in-law?"

"Not good. That's what I wanted to talk to you about."

Rooney shook his head. "I didn't think it would be easy. What happened?"

"I tried to get his version of what happened, but he didn't tell me a damned thing. He wouldn't even tell me what he does for a living. Gave me some bullshit about doing this and that."

Rooney finished the first half of his hero, took another swallow of coffee, and wiped his mouth. "I intentionally didn't fill you in on my brother-in-law. I figured that it would be better if you dug it out for yourself, but I guess that didn't work. Barney's Kathy's only sibling. He was a preemie and nearly died at birth. The Morans followed the Irish tradition of marrying late in life, and by the time they had Barney they felt that they were too old to have any more children. Needless to say, they spoiled him rotten. Nothing was too good for the little bastard, and he believes that the whole world owes him. He's too damn lazy to do any honest work *or* to learn how to better himself. My in-laws sent him to two expensive colleges, and all he learned was how to party and have a good time."

"So he has a college degree?"

Rooney shook his head. "I didn't say that. He flunked out of both of them."

"How does he support himself? I assume his parents didn't leave him filthy rich."

"Not 'filthy rich', but the dear boy does have a trust fund. Barney Moran's grandfather did very well in insurance and left the agency to my father-in-law. When he died, I represented the estate, and we sold the agency for good bucks, and that was used to fund Barney III's trust. He left everything else to Kathy's mother, and when she died her entire estate was added to the trust. The trust was discretionary. Mrs. Moran was the trustee. She was fairly generous to him, but she did hold him in check. Now Kathy's the trustee, and she's been giving him just about everything he asks for. The way I see it, the fund will run dry in a year or so."

Ian ate a few forkfuls of his chef's salad and took a sip of coffee. "Then what happens?"

"Unfortunately, I suspect Kathy'll dig into her pocketbook and continue to support him. Her grandfather left her a bundle."

"That makes sense. . . . As far as it goes."

Rooney stared at his associate. "As far as what goes?"

"I guess there are a *couple* things that don't make sense. In the first place, why does Kathy protect him so fiercely? If she kept him on a tight rein, she could force him to do some useful work."

Rooney smiled. "That's easy. Her parents both impressed on her that, as a woman, she must take care of her family. Now that her mother's gone, Kathy sees herself as Barney's mother."

". . .Okay, then—if Barney's that well fixed, why's he into loan sharking?"

"I thought that would be obvious. Pure ego. My brother-in- law thinks he's the smartest, most charming man who ever lived. I'm sure you noticed the phony Irish brogue. The stupid bastard thinks he's cute. He pals around with middle-level crime people. It makes him feel important."

CHAPTER 8

FTER COURT ON MONDAY, IAN GOT a message to call Harold Watkins. "Who's he?" he asked Rosie.

"He wouldn't say, Mr. Elkins. He didn't even tell me where he was from. He said it was personal, and he sounded like he knew you."

"The name doesn't ring a bell. Think he's a salesman?"

"Probably. If he is, he'll call again."

Sinking into his office chair, Ian wondered whether he should bother with the call. An anonymous call pretending to know you was one of the gimmicks salesmen and stock brokers used to get a foot in the door. Many people he knew discarded such messages, but he was too polite. He was about to return the call when he was summoned to Rooney's office.

At a quarter of six he was dictating papers on the project Rooney had given him when the phone rang. Since the receptionist had gone home he picked up. "Rooney and Associates."

"Ian Elkins, please," said a woman's voice.

"This is he. Who's calling?"

"Mr. Watkins wants to speak to you."

A moment later, a man's voice come on. "Hello, Ian, this is Hal Watkins."

"Hello, Mr. Watkins. Sorry I didn't get back to you sooner."

"You don't remember me, do you?"

The name *was* familiar. "Not quite."

"I worked for you for a little while when you were the articles editor of the review."

The recognition was instant: bland kid from the mid-west, an invitee on the law review, an okay worker, but he had not made it as a named editor. "Oh, yes, of course. How are you, Hal?"

"Doing fine. I'm in the general counsel's office of Universal Electronics."

"That's great. . . . Didn't I hear you'd gone with White & Case?"

". . .Yeah, I was in corporate. Universal's a good client of theirs, and they sent me over to cement their position."

Ian smiled. What the poor bastard meant was his firm decided he wasn't partnership material and farmed him out to a client. "Great company. You've got a solid future there. Probably be the next G.C."

"From your mouth to God's ears. . . . There's something I wanted to ask you."

"Fire away."

"You're involved with the Estate of Cora Kronen?"

Ian's antennae went up. "Sort of. Why?"

"Our executive V.P. asked to find out what was doing."

". . .Is that Roger Linden?"

"Yeah."

"His wife's my client. Why doesn't she call me?"

"Roger doesn't think you're pushing it hard enough."

Ian's jaw tightened. "Look, Hal, you know I can't discuss the case with you without my client's permission. Have her call me and okay it."

". . . Okay, will do."

As he heard the phone click, Ian felt sorry for the young man. He hoped Linden wouldn't get him fired.

He returned to his dictation but found it difficult go get started. Here was Barbara Linden, being pushed to go after her brother because he was probably stealing from her and her kids. And there was Kathy Rooney, vigorously protecting her crooked brother who probably wouldn't think twice about stealing from her. He thought about his own brother, Charlie, the English professor who taught Chaucer in California. Would Charlie ever steal from him? He doubted it. . .but then, what reason would there be for it? There was no real money in the Elkins family. From Charlie his thoughts turned to their mother, rotting away in the nursing home. He hadn't seen her in nearly a month. He'd better go over later in the week, but he dreaded it.

ON TUESDAY IAN DECIDED THAT, since he wasn't getting any help from his client Barney Moran, he'd better try to talk to the other side. He didn't think it would work, but he put in a call to the South Bronx Command, asked for Detective Mullins, and left a message with a desk sergeant. The next day, while he was in landlord and tenant court, his cell phone vibrated. He stepped out of the courtroom. "Hello?"

"Ian Elkins?"

"Yes. Who's this?"

"Tim Mullins, counselor. You called me yesterday."

"Yes. Thanks for calling back. It's about my client, Barney Moran."

"That wise guy? What about him?"

"I'm trying to find out what his case is about."

"It's all in the indictment."

Ian had the feeling he was being stonewalled, but he pressed on. "Come on, that doesn't tell me anything."

"I assume you asked for discovery and a bill of particulars?"

"I have, but that won't tell me everything."

"What makes you think I will?"

"I thought you Bronx cops want to be fair."

Mullins laughed. "Counselor, are you trying to bullshit me, or are you naive?"

"I guess the latter, but if you won't talk to me, at least say so."

"I didn't say *that*. If I don't talk to you, you're liable to tell a reporter on the *Post* or the *News*, and that'll make us look bad."

Ian chuckled. "So? When and where?"

The detective told him he was in criminal court, just about to testify, but should be done in half an hour, and they arranged to meet at a coffee shop across from the Criminal Courts Building.

The shop was in a narrow store with a counter running half the depth on the right. There were two booths behind the counter and eight along the left wall. Mullins was seated at the next to last booth on the left. He had medium brown hair in the process of slowly balding, was a little on the heavy side, and was dressed in a brown-and-blue checked sports jacket and an open- necked tan shirt. Seated opposite him was an attractive blonde. They were having sandwiches and soda. "Counselor, my partner, Mary Ellen Ryan."

Ian introduced himself. "I hope I'm not interfering with your lunch."

"Nah, this is the best place to see people," Mullins assured him. "The friggin' precinct's a madhouse." "I haven't seen you around the criminal courts before," said Ryan. "How'd you get involved with Barney Moran?"

"He's my boss's brother-in-law. I do just about all civil."

She tossed her hair. "You're stuck with a real loser." She looked at her watch and turned to her partner. "I've got to get back, Timmy. DA wants to talk to me before I testify in Perez. Pick up my tab, and I'll pay you later."

"Sure thing, M.E."

When the detective left, a dark-haired waitress in a stained apron came up to the table and asked Ian, "Can I get you something?"

He would have liked to order his usual chef's salad but hesitated because the place looked none too clean. Noticing this, Mullins spoke up. "The grilled cheese probably won't kill you, counselor."

"I'll take my friend's suggestion—and a cup of coffee."

"I didn't say the coffee wouldn't kill you," the detective said with a smile, and they both laughed.

When the waitress left, Mullins took a small bite of his sandwich, took a sip of soda, and looked up at Ian. "What can I tell you?

According to the indictment, Barney loaned you five thou, and a month later you paid back $5,125.00."

"So?"

"That's twenty-seven-percent interest, only two points over the legal rate. Seems kind of low for usury."

The detective shrugged. "It's over the legal rate . . . but he did tell me he was giving me a break because we were friends."

Ian was tempted to bring up Barney's claim about the extra twenty-five but decided against it. "Yeah, I understand you two grew up together. Were good friends."

"We grew up in the same neighborhood, went to Catholic school together. I guess we were friends, but I wouldn't say *good* friends."

Ian looked up at the ceiling as he pondered this distinction. It was one of old fashioned painted tin jobs with a diamond design. "Did you know the family?"

"Yeah, I knew the Morans. They had more money than we did. His older sister, Kathy, was a nice kid. In fact I almost married her best friend's kid sister, but I wasn't really that close to Barney. I don't go for loud mouthed wise guys."

Ian's sandwich and coffee arrived. He took a sip of the coffee and made a face. "You were right."

"Told you so."

Ian nodded. "Didn't he know you were a cop when he loaned you the money?"

"Sure he did, but Barney was never too bright."

Ian took a bite of his sandwich. "Right again—it's pretty good."

Mullins nodded

"Had you ever borrowed money from him before?"

"Nope. I'm not the borrowing kind. The only loan I have is the mortgage on my apartment."

"How come you borrowed money from him?"

"I told him I needed the money. That I lost a bundle in a poker game, and was afraid my wife would kill me. I said I was getting a loan from a member of my family but needed five now while he was raising the dough."

"But that wasn't so?"

"Nope, my lieutenant told me to. There's been some beatings reported around the precinct. Guys who couldn't pay back their loans. One of our snitches told us that Barney was lending dirty money at high rates. Since everybody knew that I went back a long way with the crumb, they used me to make the loan and figured that he'd make a deal and give up his sources."

"I guess he didn't go for it."

"No, he's too scared to. Why don't you talk to the DA? Maybe you can work something out."

CHAPTER 9

A T 2:45 ON A DRIZZLY THURSDAY afternoon, and Ian, who had finished lunch an hour before, was dictating into a tape recorder when the intercom buzzed. "Mrs. Linden is here for your appointment. She says she's a little early."

He made a face. "About an hour. See if she wants some coffee, show her into the library, and, if she takes a coffee, bring me one, too. I guess I wasn't meant to finish my paperwork."

Ian entered the library five minutes later and found Barbara Linden seated at the table, sipping coffee. His cup was to her left. "Your office makes excellent coffee. I must come here more often." She rose and extended her hand.

He took it with a smile. "Any time you're in the neighborhood." Slim figure, attractive double-breasted suit, and dark shiny hair—he was thinking. This is a nice woman, better than most of his visitors.

"I'm sorry to be so early, Mr. Elkins, but I finished all my errands early, and my oldest daughter is coming home from school tonight on spring break."

"I'll forgive you on one condition, Mrs. Linden."

"And that is?" She looked slightly startled.

"That you call me Ian."

"Only if you call me Barbara."

They shook hands to seal the deal, and turned to the excellent coffee.

After a silent minute, Ian decided to break the ice. "Tell me, Barbara—to what do I owe the pleasure of your visit?"

She cleared her throat. "I hate to be a pest . . . ."

". . .But?"

"But I have to know what's happening in the case."

"When we spoke about it on the phone last week, I told you that your brother's lawyer promised an informal account in two or three weeks at the most."

"I know, but . . . ."

"Roger's pressuring you."

She nodded.

"Know how I know?"

She shook her head.

"I have two sources. Your brother's lawyer called me a few days ago and told me that Roger had called him, calling your brother a thief. Then a lawyer in Roger's company's law department, whom I know slightly from law school, called me wanting to know the status. I told him I didn't have the right to give him or Roger any information without your say-so."

She winced. "What are you going to do?"

He placed his palms on the table and leaned towards her. "Exactly what I told you before. Wait one more week to see if he keeps his promise to give me an informal accounting. If

I don't get it, I'll write one more letter, and, if he still doesn't deliver, start a compulsory accounting. Then the court will require him to do it."

She frowned, scratching her cheek with her thumb. "What about the joint accounts and the power of attorney he told me about?"

Ian smiled. "We both know that the first account he gives us won't show the joint accounts. When he gives us an account without them, *then* we question him."

"Roger says he either won't answer, or he'll tell lies."

"He's right. That's exactly what I expect. Once the court requires an account, though, he's *got* to give one. Then I can depose him, let him tell his lies under oath, and pin down enough details of the lies hopefully to disprove them. But I've told you all of that before, and that's not really why you're here."

She looked puzzled.

"It's the same problem you had when you spoke to Bill Cohen and when you first came to me. It's Roger. He's very angry with your brother, he thinks he's stealing from you and your children, and he'd like to hang Herb up by his thumbs. You only came to Bill Cohen and me because Roger pushed you into it. I know you feel sorry for your brother because of the way your mother treated him. If you will recall, I originally asked you if I should also report to Roger, and you said no." He added kindly. "Are those still my instructions?"

For several minutes she was silent, deep in thought. "I'll have to give it more thought. For now, please—talk only to me."

As he returned to his room Ian smiled. Barbara is one gutsy lady. He hoped she'd be able to stand up to her husband.

LATE FRIDAY MORNING, IAN HAD just taken care of his last case in landlord-and-tenant when his cell phone vibrated. He left the courtroom and pressed the talk button. "Ian Elkins."

"Sounds like you're rehearsing for a TV drama," Rosie told him.

"Hi. What's up?"

"A Mister Jones from the DA's office called. Said your discovery in Moran was ready, thought you might want to talk to him when you pick it up."

"Thanks for calling. You saved me a trip. Would you call him and say I'm on my way over?"

He crossed over the Grand Concourse in the bright sunshine and hiked the several blocks to the criminal courts building, which had only been up for a few years and was already overcrowded. Good thing they were working on an even newer building to the east. His briefcase felt a little heavy with the L & T files he was carrying, and he wondered if he had enough room to fit in the documents he'd be picking up. He resented having to knock himself out for an uncooperative wiseguy like Barney, but decided that after all he was a client and Kathy's brother.

He got out of the elevator on the fourth floor and approached a woman with a round, pockmarked face seated at a circular receptionist desk. "Mr. Jones, please. He's expecting me."

"Which Mr. Jones?" she asked, pushing an unkempt mop of red hair away from her eyes.

". . .I don't know. Didn't know you had two. It's on the Barney Moran case."

"What kind of a case?"

"Usury."

She shook her head. "No, I mean felony or misdemeanor?"

"Felony."

"Oh, that must be Carlton Jones, he's in supreme court trials. Identification?"

Ian looked puzzled.

"You a lawyer?"

He nodded.

"Show me a picture ID."

He showed her the secure pass that enabled him to get into most courthouses without going through the metal detector.

She studied the pass and compared the picture with his face. "Sign in." She pointed to a log book on the left side of her desk and, as he did so spoke into the intercom. "Have a seat. He'll be with you shortly." She pointed to a line of eight chairs, five of which were occupied.

Sensing that it was going to be a long wait, Ian took a sip of water from a lukewarm fountain, seated himself on a hard wooden chair, and opened his briefcase.

Twenty minutes later, his concentration on a decision on page 17 of the law journal was interrupted.

"Mr. Elkins?"

He looked up at a tall, slim Black man with a medium-length goatee. "Mr. Jones?"

"Carl Jones. Come on into my office." He led Ian down a hallway with doors on both sides and into the sixth room on the right. On the right side of the door hung a framed card with the man's name. Jones seated himself behind a cluttered desk backing on the single window and motioned Ian to a seat.

Ian looked around and grinned. "I see you're one up on me."

"Beg pardon?"

"My room's the same size as yours, but you've got a window."

"Reward for serving the cause of justice," Jones replied drily, leaning back in his seat. "Come work for the good guys, maybe I can get you one."

"I used to have two when I worked for the surrogate."

"Ah, but those are all saints. . . . What's an ex-good guy doing working for slime like Barney Moran?"

"He's my boss's brother-in-law, and from what his sister tells me he's really not a bad guy. What'd he do—make one loan at a slightly inflated rate?"

Jones laughed out loud. "Try thirty-two last month. The one he made to the detective was just the tip of the iceberg, and at the lowest rate." He handed Ian a large red-rope envelope. "Here's the discovery you asked for." Jones leaned forward his palms on the desk, eyes level with Ian's. "You go to trial, your guy's going away for a long stretch."

"What's my other option?" Ian noticed a certificate on the wall showing Jones had been the notes editor on the *N.Y.U Law Review* four years after he graduated. "I see we have a history," he said, pointing. "I used to be the articles editor."

Jones smiled. "I thought your name was familiar."

"How come you're not on Wall Street, Mr. Jones?"

"Call me Carl."

"Ian."

Jones scratched his beard. "When I was growing up, I saw a lot of my friends go the wrong way. I thought that by being a prosecutor I could do some good. . . . Besides, with a little luck I can change this suit for a robe and sit on the other side of the bench. What about you? There's a good market for articles editors at the big shops."

". . . .Howard McCann."

Jones nodded. "Damned good judge."

"He convinced me I could do a lot more good working for him than for corporate fat cats."

"What made you leave?"

"Politics. I backed the wrong horse in a primary. . . . But I'm going back to the court."

"Really? When?"

"By the end of the year—I hope."

"Good luck! In the meantime, what are you going to do about Moran?"

"You have any suggestions?"

"Could be. He's only small fry, but he works for some very bad citizens. There are some people in my neighborhood who had trouble paying his bosses back and got beat up pretty bad. A guy I went to school with was nearly killed. If your guy will cooperate with us, we might be able to drop the charges down to a misdemeanor."

Ian shook his head. "Didn't the cops talk to him about that before?"

"Could be."

Ian turned sideways and leaned towards the prosecutor. "Strictly off the record, assuming he *could* testify for you— how does he stay alive afterwards?"

"Good question. Why don't you talk to the man? If he's willing to do something, maybe we can help him."

CHAPTER 10

O N THE LAST FRIDAY EVENING of spring break, the entire Linden family was gathered for dinner. Since it
was a special occasion, they were seated around the
dining room table instead of the alcove in the kitchen. Barbara was concerned that the floor was covered with the same
ecru carpeting as the adjoining living room—her middle
daughter, Marci had a penchant for upsetting filled glasses.
The teak table, which could be expanded to serve ten or
twelve, had been shortened to accommodate eight. It was set
with their best china, fine white porcelain edged in pale blue,
accompanied by crystal water and wine goblets and sterling
silverware. In the center of the table stood two silver candle-
sticks and two bottles, one of cabernet, the other of soda.

Barbara and Chelsey, her oldest daughter, rose, chanted a
blessing, and lit the candles. Roger made a blessing over the
wine and poured for Barbara and himself. He reached for
Chelsey's glass, but the tall slim brunette, with long hair like
her mother's, held up her hand. "No thanks, Dad, I really

don't like the taste. I'll stick with Coke."

"I'll have some, Dad," said the slightly plump Marci.

Roger shook his head. "You know the rules. No alcohol 'til you're eighteen."

"But, *Daddy*," she moaned, pushing curly blonde locks away from her face, "that won't be for another *year*. How can I get to be a wine connoisseur?"

"Take a wine book out of the library," Roger told her, to the amusement of the other Linden ladies.

"Besides," Chelsey added with a sneer, "wine has a lot more calories than Diet Coke, and you don't need to get any fatter."

Marci blushed as she contemplated the tight waistband on her dark brown slacks. "Thank *you*, Miss Perfect."

"That'll be quite enough, girls," said Barbara. "This is supposed to be a happy occasion."

"Sorry, Mom."

Barbara smiled. "Chelsey, would you please help me bring the food in?"

As her older sister repaired to the kitchen, Marci seethed. Why was that bitch the favorite? She *was* prettier and got better grades, but Marci was the *artistic* one—and the nice person.

Five minutes later they were eating a fresh fruit cup, followed by a green salad. Then came pot roast with green beans and roasted potatoes.

"That was great, Barbara," Roger announced when they had finished.

The three children nodded in agreement.

"What's for dessert?" Roger asked.

"Your favorite, cherry pie and vanilla ice cream."

"That sounds great," said Marci and Janie.

"May I be excused?" asked Chelsey.

"What's the matter?" Marci asked. "Afraid of putting on an ounce?"

"That will be quite enough, young lady," Roger barked. "What's up, Chelsey?"

"Billy Fine's picking me up in a few minutes, and I'd like to get ready."

She was probably going to put in her diaphragm, thought Marci. wondering what Daddy would think if he knew.

"Where are you going?"

"A party at Sally Evan's."

"Don't stay out too late," Roger warned her.

By eight, all three children were out of the house—Chelsey on her date, Marci to a movie with girlfriends, and Janie at a sleep-away party. Roger had helped Barbara with the final stages of cleanup, and they were snuggled on the living room couch, sipping their second cups of coffee and listening to Mantovani classics on the CD player.

"Not that I don't love my children, but this is nice," she purred.

"Mm!" he replied, rubbing the back of her neck.

Fifteen minutes later, the coffee cups were empty. "Want a refill?" she asked.

"Not now—but I could go for something else."

"I wonder what he means by that."

He chuckled.

"Could you have an *activity* in mind?"

He nodded.

"One better performed upstairs?"

He smiled and assisted her to rise. ". . .By the way, there's something I've been meaning to ask you."

"Yes?"

"I've been trying to get a status report from your lawyer on the case against your brother, but the guy won't talk to me or my company lawyer."

She let out a breath. "Please, Roger, this could be a very lovely evening. Don't spoil it."

As soon as Ian returned from his visit to the DA's office, he immediately dictated a memorandum of the meeting and had his secretary make a copy of the discovery for Rooney. By the end of the afternoon he had skimmed the discovery, and he was halfway through a thorough reading when Rooney summoned him to his office. He found the boss drinking coffee and chomping on chocolate coated donuts. A cup of hot black coffee was opposite the middle visitor's chair.

"Thanks, Mark, I could use this," he said, sitting down and taking a swallow.

"So what do you think?" Rooney asked, pointing to his copy of the discovery.

Ian shook his head. "I'm not finished with it yet, but from what I've read so far, they've got Barney by the short hairs."

"That's my impression, too. What do you think we should do?"

Ian chuckled. "The impossible." He noticed Rooney's incredulous expression. "What I mean is, make a deal which, under Kathy's ultimatum, is impossible."

Rooney smiled. "I think we're turning you into an Irish stand-up comic. . . .Let me talk to Kathy tonight and insist that she have the bum come in for a conference. I know he's been ducking you."

"You don't want to have Kathy in on the meeting, do you?" Ian asked with a worried expression.

"I know the attorney-client privilege doesn't extend to lawyer's wives or client's sisters. You don't think I'm going senile?"

"No way, boss." Ian tried to hide his relief.

"I assume the DA is offering witness protection."

"That's the way I read it."

"Can he do it?"

"I think so. From what I've read, the act can apply to state crimes that are like federal ones, and this one seems like RICO. I guess they'll have to go to the U.S. Attorney and ask for it."

Rooney devoured nearly half a fresh donut. "Okay. I'll have Kathy set up the meeting. I want you to continue to go over the discovery. By the time of the meeting, I'll expect you to know it by heart and be able to cite chapter and verse."

ROONEY PULLED HIS BURGUNDY MERCEDES onto the driveway of his four-bedroom colonial in Hartsdale a little after 6:00. It was still light out; he waited for a moment to admire the white columns surrounding the front entrance. While he hadn't grown up poor, his parents could never have afforded such a house.

He pulled the car into the three-car garage, removed his briefcase, and entered the mud room that led to the kitchen. Kathy, in faded jeans and a tank top, was seated at the big breakfast table sipping chai and reading a popular novel. As he came, he caught the aroma of a carrot cake in the oven.

She started as she heard him enter. "What are you doing home so early? Expect to catch me with my boyfriend, or did you smell the cake all the way down in the Bronx?"

"Can't a man come home early to his beautiful wife without being made fun of?" Beautiful was an understatement, he thought as he kissed her.

She beamed and kissed him back. "Don't kid a kidder. I'm no more beautiful today than I was yesterday or will be tomorrow."

"Well, there *was* something I wanted to discuss, . . . but it'll keep 'til after dinner."

She shook her head. "Like hell it will. Get us a drink and we'll talk about it now. . . . It *is* about Barney?" she continued as he headed to the bar.

"Kathleen, you are a sorceress."

She laughed. "No, *you* are an open book."

Five minutes later they were seated at the table with drinks in front of them. She tasted her old fashioned. "Spill it!"

For the next ten minutes, between sips of Irish over ice, he filled her in on what Ian had learned. "I guess you'll want to come into the office and hear it from the horse's mouth."

She shook her head. "No. You're right. He's got to make a deal. I'll talk to him. But—" she concluded, fixing him with her pale-green eyes—"make *sure* that he gets the kind of witness protection that'll keep him alive."

CHAPTER 11

THAT MOVIE WAS GREAT," SALLY SAID. "Yeah," Herb agreed. "I never laughed so hard. Nearly split my sides."

When he pulled the Pontiac into the driveway of her co-op, the doorman came out and opened her door. "Good evening, Miss Martinis."

"Hi, Larry."

"They always stick you with weekends?" Herb asked.

"Most of the time, but I don't have seniority yet."

"It'll come," she said. "Even *this* guy's gotten some promotions. . . . By the way, can you keep Herb's car in Visitors for a while?"

He hesitated for a moment. "For a little while. The manager doesn't like visitors cars here all night."

"No problem. If someone from management comes around, call up and remind us that you called before and we have to get the car out *pronto*. Don't worry, the manager's my friend. We'll make it worth your while."

Herb leaned over and whispered into her ear. "Hey, I've got to be at work early tomorrow, and I have to finish the accounting for Mom's estate."

"Just come up for an hour." She kissed him.

"I'll be back in a little while," he said as he opened the driver's side door.

"Sure thing, Mr. Kronen," the doorman replied with a knowing smile.

They took the elevator to the twenty-seventh floor, and Sally opened the third door on the right. He smiled. "This apartment has class."

"It's okay, I guess."

"Better than mine."

She shrugged. "That doesn't take much."

"You've got two bedrooms."

"The small one barely holds my desk and computer."

"The living room and the master bedroom are nice sized."

She frowned. "Bedroom's okay, but I wish I had a separate dining room. . . . I've got to make a siss. Get us some drinks."

He half chuckled at the word little girls at school used. "What're you having?"

"The usual," she replied heading for the bathroom.

When she returned he noticed she had taken off her jeans and blouse and was wearing a peach-colored silk kimono. She seated herself next to him on a cream-colored sofa . Her Manhattan and his coffee were on the cocktail table in front of them. "Nice," she said after taking a sip. "You only drinking coffee?"

"I told you, I've got to be at the office early, and I wanted to work on the estate accounting before I went to sleep."

"You still doing *that*?"

"Got some problems."

"Like what?"

"What to do about the joint accounts. There's too much."

She shook her head. "Herb—that's the *idea*. They've *got* to be big enough so you have room to settle."

"That's what Harley keeps telling me."

"He's right." She downed the balance of her drink, reached over, and ran her fingers over the front of his pants. "Now come on, I need some exercise."

As she rose from the couch she took his left hand and pulled him to his feet. He shrugged and hugged her. Well, he thought, he needed it, too.

To get from the kitchen to the dining room Chez Rooney, it is necessary to cross the rear end of the living room. Early Tuesday evening the table was set for two. "That was wonderful, Kathy. My favorite, and a touch of the old sod." Barney pushed aside an empty plate that had been heaped with loin of pork in a white sauce with sauerkraut and mashed potatoes.

"You sure I can't get you more?"

"I couldn't fit another morsel."

"Not even carrot cake with ice cream and Irish coffee?"

He looked up at his sister with a near angelic expression. "Now, sure and it would be disrespectful if I allowed your delicious carrot cake to go to waste, so give me just a wee sliver."

Kathy cut a large piece, put it on a plate, added two scoops of vanilla ice cream, and set it in front of him. "Why don't you start on this while I get the coffee?"

He smiled broadly as he dug in. "I don't deserve to have

an angel like you for my sister."

She silently agreed as she went into the kitchen.

A few minutes later brother and sister settled down in the living room with the coffees. Barney was leaning back in his brother-in-law's favorite recliner; Kathy sat on the edge of one of the straight-backed armchairs. "So, dear sister of mine." The sentence was punctuated by a belch. "I certainly appreciate the feast, but what's the occasion?"

"Can't a girl feed her favorite brother?"

"Of course, though I notice the absence of the lord of the manor. Is it possible that the lady is contemplating incest?"

She laughed. "Behave yourself, Barney. . . . You are right, however, in supposing that I have something to discuss with you."

"Spill it, then," he replied with feigned alarm. "Don't keep me in suspense."

The smile slowly evaporated from her face. "Barney, this is serious. Mark isn't here for a good reason. He doesn't want to be present when I talk with you for fear of jeopardizing your attorney-client privilege. I just fed you that meal for a good reason. I want you to realize that this isn't the kind of food they'll be serving you in state prison."

His pixyish expression turned somber. "What're you talking about? I didn't do anything that could put me in *prison*. I may have done a few undeserving people a favor, but that's all."

She stared at him. "Barney, that's a lot of crap. I've been told enough to know that they've got the goods on you. Mark said they've performed their discovery, and they can prove their case against you with your own documents. If you go to trial, you're going to be convicted on a first-degree count, and they can send you away for fifteen years. I know you work for some very bad people, though, and that's really why they're after you. If you take a plea and testify against them, you can get a good deal—maybe no jail time at all."

Barney shook his head. "Kathy, you don't understand. These people are friends, but if I were to turn on them, my life wouldn't be worth a plugged nickel."

She let out a breath. "Your so-called friends can't keep you out of jail. . . . Barney, you can get witness protection. . . . Go in and talk to Mark and Ian. I don't want to have to visit you in prison."

CHAPTER 12

O N Wednesday Ian called Goldberg's office to press for the accounting. He left word on the man's voice mail. When he received no response, he called again the next day and followed it up with a letter by certified mail. On Monday he got a message that Goldberg had returned his call, and, he finally reached him on Tuesday.

"Why the hell are you bugging me, *Counselor*?"

"I'm not bugging you, Mr. Goldberg. You promised me an informal accounting nearly a month ago. When will I get it?"

Goldberg smiled. "Why should I bother giving you an informal? You're only going to go for a compulsory anyway."

Ian bristled. "Fine. I'll see you in court."

"Wait a minute, *sonny*, I didn't say I wouldn't give you one."

Ian snapped the lead in the pencil he was using. "When do I *get* it?"

"Soon."

"Not good enough."

Goldberg mentally counted to ten. "I just got it in from the client yesterday. I want to look it over before I send it out."

WHEN HE GOT BACK FROM COURT on Monday Ian asked Rosie whether the accounting had come. "In this morning's mail. Mr. Rooney has it, and he'd like to speak to you."

"I see you have a tray ready."

She nodded.

"Would you add a cup of coffee for me, please?"

"Your wish is my command," she replied with a bow.

"Hi, Mark, what's up?" he asked as he seated himself in the middle visitor's chair and stared at the clothesline through the window directly behind his boss.

Rooney looked up from his papers. "You see Rosie? I asked her for some coffee and a few cookies."

Ian suppressed a smile. "I'm afraid I caused the delay. I asked her to add a coffee for me."

"No problem, so long as she didn't forget."

"I hear you got the accounting in Kronen."

"Yeah." Rooney passed over a number ten envelope. "I thought you told me this was a six-million-dollar estate."

"That's what Bill Cohen told me."

"How come this only shows three-million-five?"

"The client thinks her brother got the proceeds from joint accounts."

"How're you going to find out?"

"I'll ask the lawyer for a copy of the 706."

"Huh?"

"You know, the federal estate tax return."

"Oh, yeah. . . . Will he give it to you?"

"If not, the court will order it."

"That guy, Goldberg, is one cocky bastard."

"He is. What makes you say so?"

"Didn't you see his letter?" Rooney extracted it from the envelope, handed it to Ian, and pointed. "He sent along a release and expects the client to sign it."

"WHAT'S NEW AND EXCITING?" MOLLY asked as the family waited for their Friday night dinner.

"*Hey*. That's *my* line," Sam insisted.

"Who gave it to you?" Molly demanded.

"It's my right as the head of this family."

"And who made you the head?"

"I'm the oldest man *here*." He pounded his fist into his palm for emphasis.

"Now I've heard everything," Helen interjected. "My father a *chauvinist*?"

"You mean you didn't know?" Eric asked.

"Hey, whose side are you on?" Sam demanded.

"Mommy, what's a sho. . . ?" Carol asked.

"Chauvinist, dear. That's a man who thinks he's better than us women."

"Does Grampa think he's . . . one of those?"

Helen repeated the word slowly and added, "No, we're just joking."

"Besides, he wouldn't dare," Molly concluded." She turned towards Ian. "*So?*"

"What?"

"What I asked you before Mr. Big Shot butted in."

Helen tapped him on the shoulder. "Mom wants to know

what's new and exciting?"

He turned towards her and stroked her expanding middle. "This is new and exciting."

"Yes," Carol piped up. "That's my new brother or sister. . . . Which is it going to be?"

"That's what makes it new and exciting," Ian replied. "We won't know 'til we do."

Carol giggled.

Molly cleared her throat. "I meant new and exciting in the *law*."

"Nothing, but I had an interesting development in the estate accounting case I told you about."

"Good," Sam demanded. "Tell us about it,"

Molly rose from her chair and pointed a finger at her husband's nose. "I beg your pardon, Mr. Big Shot, but I thought I was asking this set of questions."

Sam put up his hands in surrender.

"Tell us about it," Molly continued in triumph.

"If you'll remember," Ian continued. "The accounting he submitted showed only a little over half the assets we knew the old lady had. So I asked for a copy of the 706."

"That's the federal estate tax return," Sam explained.

Molly glared at him. "How long have I been the wife of an accountant?"

"Sorry."

"Did you get it?"

"Yes I did, Mom."

"And?"

"And there was a two-and-a-half-million item in joint accounts going to the son."

"What'll you do next?" asked Eric.

"I wrote the lawyer a letter demanding copies of all documents involved in the setting up of the joint accounts including any powers of attorney used."

"You get them?" asked Sam.

"Tune in next Friday night for the continuing saga."

"Dinner's ready, Mrs. K.," announced a voice from the kitchen.

THE FOLLOWING MONDAY AT 2:30 Ian and Rooney had just finished lunch and were drinking coffee. Rooney looked at his watch. "Where the hell is that guy?"

Ian took the last sip of his coffee and looked at the foam cup. Maybe one of these days he'd buy a silver-colored ceramic one and have it marked *Assistant Boss*. "What did you expect, Mark? Has Barney ever been on time?"

Rooney scratched his jaw. "Well, he got to the church only ten minutes late for my wedding, and we were able to squeeze him into the procession. But I did have you schedule this for 1:30 so he'd be here by 2:00." At that moment the intercom buzzed. "Yes, Rosie?"

"Mr. Moran is here for his appointment."

"Send him in," Rooney growled.

A minute later, Barney sidled into the room, attired in a silver-toned double-breasted suit, a black shirt, a white tie, and tasseled loafers. "How are you, my dear brother-in-law?" He shook Rooney's hand, patted Ian on the back and sat down next to him.

"When the fuck did you join the Mafia?" Rooney demanded with a scowl.

Barney looked puzzled, then smiled. "Oh, you mean my glad rags. They were perfectly appropriate for the last St.

Paddy's Day Parade."

"Where've you been? We made a date for one-thirty."

"Oh, dear, and I thought I was early. I missed my lunch."

Rooney picked up the phone, but didn't press the intercom. "Rosie, order Mr. Moran an arsenic sandwich on rye."

"If it's all the same to you, Mark, could you make it on a roll?"

As Ian watched the show, he found it nearly impossible to keep from laughing.

Rooney gritted his teeth. "Can we get on with this?"

Barney gave him a sly smile. "Of course. Kathy said you wanted to see me, so here I am."

"And she told you what it was about?"

"She said something about my case."

"And that's all she said?"

He feigned concentration. "I think so."

"*Bullshit*! Ian, tell this guy what you've learned."

For the next half hour Ian filled him in. As the big man listened, his amusement faded to acute concern. "Let me get this straight. What you're telling me is that, if we go to trial I'll get fifteen years in the state pen?"

"Not exactly. My guess is that, since it's your first felony conviction, you'll probably pull ten-to-twelve, and, if you behave yourself, be out in six-to-eight,"

". . .What do I do?"

"If you testify against your bosses, they'll drop it down to a misdemeanor, and you probably won't serve more than a few months."

"But Ian, they're my *friends*. . . . Besides, if I rat on them, I'll be *dead*."

"As I told you, we'll only let you testify if you get witness protection."

"I thought that was only for federal cases."

"That's what I thought too, but since I started on this case, I've learned a few things. In the first place, New York also has witness protection."

"Is it any good?"

"In some cases, it's okay. They could move you to another borough. That'd work if this was a local street crime."

Barney frowned. "What good is that?"

"That's not what we're looking for. In a crime like yours the feds can give you federal witness protection for a state crime. From what I understand, loan sharking fits into federal racketeering, so they might offer you the good stuff."

"And what's that?"

"Change your name, get you new ID, move you to a different state, get you housing, a job."

"Probably in a store. . . . That don't sound too hot. . . . I don't guess Kathy could send me my trust money."

"Not a good idea," said Ian. "It'd probably lead them right to you."

"Look," Rooney added, "a crappy job's better than a long jail stretch."

Barney let out a breath. "This can't be happening. My friends won't let me down. I've got to talk to them."

"For God's *sake*! Don't do *that*!" Rooney shouted. "If they get the impression you're thinking about talking, they'll kill you."

Barney shook his head. "Come on, Mark, I'm not that stupid. I know how to talk to them."

"Don't do it, Barney. It's too big a risk."

"Fear not, old son, I know what I'm doing. . . . When do

I have to let you know about making a deal?"

"As soon as possible," replied Ian. "Your trial comes up in a few weeks."

"I'll let you know in a few days," Barney concluded as he rose, shook their hands, and departed.

"Christ, I can use a drink," Rooney said when they were alone. "That stupid sonofabitch is going to get himself murdered."

"What can *we* do?"

"Maybe Kathy can talk some sense into him."

CHAPTER 13

S ALLY MARTINIS RETURNED TO HER office at 2:15. The lunch meeting had gone well. If she landed the client, her mid-year bonus would rise considerably. She settled back onto her black leather manager's chair and kicked off her three-and-a-half-inch spiked heels. They really made her feet hurt and she was much more comfortable in two-inchers or even flats, but the super-high heel made her legs look fuck-me great, and experience had taught her that a man with an erection was a much easier sale. You even had to come through sometimes, but so what? . . . Though most of them weren't as well endowed as Herb. She looked around her room. Ten-by-thirteen in Rockefeller Center wasn't too bad. A couple of windows would be nice, but it was a hell of a lot better than the work station she had been given when she started at the agency. Besides, the Maynard Dixon reproductions that covered three of the walls made the room look fairly attractive. The intercom buzzed. "Yes, Emma."

"Mr. Goldberg's on three,. . .Miss Martinis."

She'd have to teach the dumb broad that the appropriate form of address was Ms. "Yes, Harley How're you doing?"

"Just great, Sal. How's our boyfriend?"

"You should know. He's your client."

"Actually, he's what I want to talk to you about."

She scribbled two stars on the legal pad on her desk pull-out. "What's the matter?"

"I'd rather discuss it in person."

"How about a few drinks at Aldo's? I'm meeting Herb there for dinner at seven-thirty."

"I'd rather he not see us together."

"Oh?" She scribbled three pound signs on the pad.

"Look, I'm in court in Manhattan. I should be done by four- thirty. What say I meet you at the place around the corner from your office?"

"Sure. What time?"

"I should be there by a quarter after five. If I'm going to be late, I'll call your cell."

AT TEN AFTER FIVE SALLY WAS starting on her third Manhattan at a crowded bar restaurant on West Forty-seventh when Harley appeared. She'd left work early in order to snag the next to last of the ten two-seat tables that ringed the barroom.

He pecked her on the cheek, signaled the bar waitress, and five minutes later was working on a double Jack Daniels on the rocks. "You're looking good."

She smiled. "You, too. New suit?"

"Yeah, a guy from a Hong Kong tailor's been calling and bugging me to try him out. A few months ago he caught me in the office, and I decided to give him a shot. Came out pretty good?"

She nodded. "I've never seen you in a double-breasted suit before."

"First I've ever had."

"Get more. It looks good on you."

He smiled broadly. "I just ordered two more."

She took a sip of her drink. "What was it you wanted to talk about?"

He crunched a handful of peanuts. "Herb."

She eyed him, reached for the peanut bowl, but stopped. "What's he done?"

"You remember he was going to put together an accounting?"

"Yeah. I sent him home a few Sundays ago to finish the job. . . . Didn't he do it?"

"He did. Got it to me on Wednesday."

"So?"

"You recall we got him to make four of his mother's accounts joint?"

"Yeah. It got him two and half mil when she died. He used the power to do it."

"Uhh. . . . Jerk's trying to change his mind."

She frowned. "How?"

"The accounting he sent me put three of the accounts back. He only kept the fourth one with the five hundred."

"That's crazy! Didn't he show the four accounts in the 706?"

Harley tossed off half his drink. "I know. His cover letter said he was going to amend the 706."

"He's out of his fucking mind. What's he gonna use for bargaining—did you talk him out of it?"

He shook his head. "I tried something a little different."

"What?"

"I changed the paperwork and sent it to his sister's lawyer."

"Does he *know*?"

He shook his head. "You've got to talk to him."

"*How*?"

"That's what we've got to figure out."

ON A WEDNESDAY MORNING IN June, the temperature was predicted to hit the nineties. Ian was seated in the front row, waiting for his case to be called, glad that he was in surrogate's court for a change. While Mark's office had given him a good grounding in L & T, he much preferred estates. Besides, the air conditioning was working much better, and it was good to schmooze with his court buddies. Donald Greene, who had been the court officer when he worked there, was as cheery as ever, although Ian had heard he was scheduled to retire at the end of the year. Sandy Jenkens was representing the Public Administrator. He'd been on staff when Ian was with the court, but had recently acquired the top spot as the first African American attorney for the Public Administrator.

Ian's case was number seven on the probate calendar, a routine estate in which no objections were anticipated, but case number two before the surrogate seemed to be causing a stir. Mike Bono, the attorney for the petitioner, usually a rock-calm estates practitioner, was arguing with three young people when the judge silenced them and spoke up. "Mr. Elkins, are you available to be appointed a guardian ad litem?"

"Yes, Your Honor," the young man replied, awakening from his reverie.

"Go into my robing room and conference it with Mr.

Crowley."

"Your Honor, I have the Brennan Estate, case number seven, to answer."

"I'll call it now," Surrogate Bill Anderson replied.

The case was called. As expected, no one appeared in opposition, and, thirty seconds later, Ian left the well of the court, turned left, and went through a door behind the judge's bench and into the robing room. "Good morning, Your Honor," he said to the overweight man seated behind the judge's massive rectangular desk, which took up about a quarter of the twelve-by- fifteen foot room.

"From your mouth to God's ears," Ian's long-time friend Herb Crowley replied.

"Is there a fix in against me?" asked Mike Bono who, but for strenuous dieting, could have been mistaken for Crowley's twin.

"Of course," replied Crowley. "Didn't you know?"

The three lawyers laughed, and the court attorney cleared his throat and turned toward the three young people who were gathered on the left side of the room. "I think I should disabuse you of the wrong impression we've obviously given you. Mr. Elkins," he continued pointing, "has just been appointed guardian ad litem of—" he looked at the court file—"Terry Keller. I've worked in the courts with Mr. Elkins for many years. Mr. Bono is a very active practitioner in this court, and he, Mr. Elkins, and I have worked together on many matters. The judge also knows both of them quite well, and I can assure you that neither of them will get favored treatment as against the other. Now, you two," he went on, indicating a tall slim man in his mid twenties and an attractive dark-haired woman in her late twenties or early thirties, "are also children of the decedent, your mother. Mr. Bono represents your father and is seeking to probate a will claimed to be your mother's that leaves everything to him and nothing to you. Since Mr. Elkins represents only your brother, Terry, you two—uh, Barry and Angela—may want to hire attorneys, and I strongly suggest that you do. In that event the judge will treat your attorney equally with Mr. Elkins and Mr. Bono. . . . Does everyone understand that?"

They nodded.

Ian took a fast look at the file, then looked up. "I see that the decedent is Mary Doyle, but that you three are named Keller. How's that?"

Mike Bono spoke up. "They lived together as husband and wife for some thirty years, and she had three children by him, but they were never officially married."

"Any idea why she left everything to him and nothing to her children?"

"I guess she figured he'd take care of his children," replied Bono.

"Like hell she did," the young woman snapped. "He made her do it. He used to beat the hell out of her."

Both of the siblings nodded.

"Come on, Angela, you know that's not true," said Bono.

She looked at him scornfully.

"This isn't the time or place to discuss the dirty laundry," said Ian. "I've got to qualify and investigate the case. Let's adjourn it for a month."

"Way too long. There's nothing to it. I've got to start administering this estate. We've some real estate to sell."

Herb Crowley held up his hand. "A month seems perfectly reasonable. I'm sure the judge'll go along."

As they left the robing room, Bono pulled Ian aside. "Look, you're certainly entitled to investigate, but there's nothing *there*. If you go along, we won't have to waste a lot of money on litigation. My client is willing to give the kid fifteen thou if there are no objections."

"Gee, Mike, that's awfully generous to his son," Ian drawled.

"He's a snotty kid, but the old man will take care of him."

Ian shrugged. "We'll see."

As Herb Crowley had predicted, the case was adjourned for a month, and after arranging to meet with the Kellers on Friday, Ian signed the required qualification papers and returned to his office.

THAT AFTERNOON HE WAS SUMMONED to the command post. "What's up, Mark?" he asked, eyes drawn to the mound of chocolate ice cream slowly melting in a bowl at Rooney's left.

"I just heard from Kathy. She's been in touch with her brother, and he's agreeable to make a deal if he can get grade-A witness protection."

"That's great."

Rooney nodded and shoveled ice cream down his throat. "That's the good part of it."

"And?"

"She wasn't able to stop him from talking with his bosses. They told him they'd do something for him, but that he'd have to tough it out."

"Think they suspect?"

"He says no, but I can't believe it, and neither does Kathy. Talk to the DA and see what you can work out."

CHAPTER 14

O N HOT FRIDAY NIGHTS THE Kaplan chicken dinner was most often cold chicken salad. The evening before Freddie Goldstein's departure for summer camp was no exception, the main course a chicken fruit salad with pineapple, grapes, orange segments, walnuts, and cut-up strawberries, served over rice with a balsamic vinaigrette. Fruit sherbets followed.

Ian declared himself blissfully sated.

"Can I get you some more?" asked Molly, dipping into the serving bowl.

"He doesn't need any more," said Helen.

"Aw, come on, sweetie, let me say it for myself. Mom, she's right, I couldn't fit another mouthful."

"Okay, *boychick*," declared Sam. "It's time to sing for your supper."

"I didn't know you had a cabaret license," Said Ian.

"Don't be a wise guy. You know the price of dinner is one of your stories about the law."

"Please, Sam," said Molly. "Hold up on the entertainment until we have our coffee in the living room. That way, Stella can clean up and get home to her husband."

Sam nodded, and they settled in the living room. He took a sip of his after-dinner brandy and turned to his son-in-law. "So?"

Ian placed his coffee mug on one of the coasters Molly had scattered around the room, stifled a smile, and began. "I don't know whether this is new and exciting. I think it's kind of sad. A few days ago my friend the surrogate appointed me a guardian ad litem in a probate case."

"Doesn't sound too sad to me," said Eric. "You'll probably make a good fee out of it."

Sam motioned for silence.

"The will of the woman who died leaves everything to a man she calls her husband and nothing to her three children, whom he fathered. She lived with the man for over thirty years, but they never got married. From what the children told me, he was and still is married to another woman and has several children by her. They said that he frequently came home drunk, beat up their mother, and wrecked the place. Daughter said the woman was scared to death; that her mother's last pregnancy, which produced the kid I represent, was very difficult; that she was in very bad shape for at least a month after the birth, stayed in bed most of the time; and that she and the baby had to be taken care of by the daughter—the claimed will was dated a week and a half after the kid was born."

"Doesn't that raise a question of lack of testamentary capacity?" asked Helen.

"Aha!" Eric exclaimed. "The estates paralegal to the rescue."

"Well, doesn't it?" she repeated.

Ian hesitated, scrambling for a tactful answer that would prevent a probate tale from turning into the storyteller's matrimonial problem. "Testamentary capacity is certainly one of the issues in the case, but it's far from a be all or end all."

"How come?"

"In the first place, you don't need much to have testamentary capacity. It's the lowest kind. Basically you have to know approximately what you have and who would be the usual objects of your bounty. Also there's a presumption that everyone who makes a will has it, so the presumption has to be overcome, and the testimony of a girl in her early teens probably wouldn't be admitted into evidence. I'd like to get testimony from the mother's obstetrician, but the daughter has no idea who her mother's doctors were."

"What about the witnesses to the will?" asked Sam. "What do they say?"

"That's another problem. There were two witnesses. One's dead, and the other can't be found. According to an affidavit from the son of the lawyer who drew the will, his father died a few months after the date of the will. The will was signed in a real estate office, where the other witness worked. The son, who's also a lawyer, can identify both his father's signature and that of the other witness. And since there was an attestation clause in the will saying the execution was supervised by a lawyer, there's a presumption that it was done right."

Sam took a sip of his brandy then shook his head. "You got a tough one!"

THAT SUNDAY NIGHT, THE TEMPERATURE remained brutally hot. Sally and Herb were attached side by side on her bed pumping away at breakneck speed. Though the bedroom air conditioning was running full blast, they were bathed in sweat. Seventeen minutes into the exercise they achieved an explosive, and near simultaneous, orgasm and collapsed, gasping, into each other's arms. God, thought Herb.

Ten minutes later, they peeled themselves off the bed and repaired to the bathroom. Later still, after a mutual shower, seated naked on towels at the kitchen table, they tried to replace their spent bodily fluids with tall glasses of iced tea.

"I'd say we did pretty good," she declared, rising to refill the glasses.

"Damned well. You are something else. If fucking was an Olympic event, you'd have a roomful of medals."

She smiled dreamily. "You're pretty good yourself. When we finish this," she said, lifting her glass, "want to go for a daily double?"

He shook his head. "Love to, but I've got to finish up something tonight."

She stared at him disappointed. "Can't you do it in the office?"

He shook his head. "It's not office work, and it's busy season at the office."

"Then put it off for a while. Is it that important?"

"Sort of. It's for the estate."

"I thought Harley does most of that."

"But not the accounting."

She forced her brow to knit. "Didn't you finish the informal accounting weeks ago?"

"Yeah, but now I've got to dovetail the 706 into those figures."

"I thought you took the accounting *from* the 706."

He shifted uncomfortably. "I was going to . . . but then I decided to make some changes."

"What changes?" she asked with a poker face.

"Uh. . .the joint accounts."

She frowned. "What *about* the joint accounts?"

He coughed and took a sip of the iced tea. "You know I didn't have the right to use the power of attorney to benefit myself. So I listed some of the joint accounts as convenience accounts and put them into the estate. I'm going to change the 706 to show that."

She starred daggers at him. "Just how much did you put back into the estate?"

"Two million. I kept five hundred." Sensing she was about to lace into him, he held up his hand. "Look, Sal, we both knew I couldn't keep the whole two-and-a half-mil. I just figured that my sister wouldn't fight me over five hundred."

She looked at him and shook her head. "I thought you Jewish accountants were smart. Do you remember what we discussed before your mother died?"

He nodded sheepishly. "Yeah. We figured we'd settle with Barbara for three-quarters-of-a-mil. . . . But that's too much. Roger would never let me get away with that, but I'm pretty sure Barbara'll let me have the five hundred."

Her head continued to shake. "Do you think Roger will let her settle for five hundred if that's *all* you take? That's why you took the two-and-a-half-mil."

"You're right, but what can I do? The cat's out of the bag. They already have the accounting. I can't change it."

His hangdog expression nearly made her comfort him, but

she let him suffer for a full minute before she smiled. "You know, you're very lucky you have a good lawyer and a good friend?"

He looked quizzical until she told him that Harley had removed all the joint accounts from the informal before he sent it out. Herb breathed a sigh of relief.

She allowed him to take another sip of iced tea, removed the glass from his hand, pushed it to the middle of the table, and led him back into the bedroom.

IAN HAD MADE A DATE WITH Carlton Jones for the following Monday at 3:30. At the receptionist's desk, he was told to go right into Jones's office. He found the door open and the man seated behind his desk, going over papers. "Welcome back," he said, looking up and extending his hand. "I was beginning to wonder if your client was going to be foolish enough to get himself fifteen years."

"Always good to visit where you're welcome." Ian seated himself in the only empty visitor's chair, looked over the man's head, and shook his head.

Jones frowned. "You mean you're not here to make a deal?"

"What makes you say that?"

"Body language. Why'd you shake your head?"

"I just decided that it wouldn't be smart to ask my boss for one of his windows, to come up even with you."

The DA laughed. "I like a kidder. What can I do for you?"

"I'm here to make a deal—*if* you can guarantee that my client will stay alive."

"Till what age?"

"How about a hundred?"

"Hey, what say we give up the law and form a comedy team?"

Ian grinned. "I've often thought about that, Carl, but I have a suspicion I'd starve to death, along with my wife and kids."

"Know what you mean. How many you got?"

"One, and one on the way."

"You're a piker. I've got three and twins on the way."

"Wow!"

Jones scratched his beard. "Okay—I've spoken to my contact at the U.S. Attorney's office. They want your guy's bosses even more than I do. Assuming he can give us what we want and testifies well, they'll give him federal witness protection."

"Meaning?"

"You're not very trusting."

"Should I be?"

"I'm going to enjoy working with you. Okay, let me lay it out. They'll change his name. Give him a new social, and a new passport. Move him somewhere, probably the mid-West. Get him housing and a job. In other words, the whole ball of wax."

"What kind of a job? He's going to ask that."

"Probably a salesman in a store like Walmart. What's he expect, CEO of a Fortune 500 company?"

"Probably. . . . Let me know when you want me to bring him in. I assume that what he says will be off the record unless we make a deal?"

"Positively. I'll work something out with the feds and call you."

CHAPTER 15

A S IAN REACHED THE OFFICE after court he was met by a frantic Rosemary Lennon. "Didn't you get my *calls*?" She rose and tugged at her slightly snug size sixteen and a half plum colored dress, trying without success to make it hang right.

"I felt my cell vibrate a few times, but I couldn't pick it up. I was in the middle of trying the Dunlop L & T. What's the problem?"

"It's Barney Moran. He's been calling every half hour. He's in jail."

"That can't *be*. He's out on bail, and he hasn't missed any court dates. Does Mark know anything about it?"

She shook her head. "No, he's on trial in Brooklyn."

"You have a number I can reach Barney?"

"No, but I'm sure he'll be calling in a few minutes."

Ian had just sat down behind his cluttered desk when the intercom buzzed. "Who is it Rosie—Barney?"

"No, it's Mrs. Rooney."

"Hi, Kathy. I just heard. Have you spoken to him?"

"He just got off the phone with me, and he's terrified. How could you let this *happen* to him?"

"I'm not sure *what* happened. I'm going to check on it and let you know. Do you have a phone number I can reach him at?"

"He didn't have the number, but he's being processed now so you can't reach him. He's going to call me later, and I'll get you the number. I'll probably visit him tonight."

"Let me call the DA. I'll get back to you."

He immediately called Jones, but the man was out. By six forty-five he had left three more messages and received two more demanding calls from Kathy. He was about to leave the office when the phone rang. "Rooney and Associates."

"Still there, Ian? I didn't think you civil lawyers put in that kind of hours."

"Carl?"

"Who else you been burning up the phone lines for?"

"Carl, what happened? My guy is in *jail*. I thought we made a *deal*."

"We did."

"Then why was he arrested?"

"To keep the stupid bastard alive 'til he testifies. Did you listen to what he told us yesterday?"

"Yeah, he told you what you needed for a conviction."

"What else?"

He scrunched his brow. "What do you mean?"

"He spoke to his bosses."

"Yeah, but they couldn't help him. He said he didn't let on that he planned to make a deal with you."

"You don't believe they'd catch on?"

Ian sighed. "...I guess you're right."

"We had to put him away so he'd live 'til trial."

"Why didn't you tell *me* first? ... Cause I'd have to tell him, and he'd skip and get killed."

"*Right*."

"Where is he?"

"Metro Correctional. It's a federal lockup on Park Row."

"Can he get visitors?"

"He can see *you*."

"What about his sister?"

"I think so. I'll call and make sure. Have her call me in half an hour."

Ian thanked him and hung up. He didn't relish making the call to Kathy.

IN COURT THE NEXT DAY, IAN'S cell vibrated. "Yeah?"

"Hi, Mr. Elkins. This is Angela Keller. I've got to see you."

"What's the matter? Is Terry alright?"

"Physically. It's my friggin' father. He's off a wall."

"I'm available late this afternoon. Who'll be with you?"

"Just me. I'll be there."

As he hung up the phone, Ian wondered whether he was getting into a conflict of interest with his ward. He told himself he'd solve the problem if it came up.

At four-thirty he was busily poring over a file and was about to dictate into his tape recorder when the intercom buzzed. "Ms. Keller is here to see you. Says she has an appointment."

"She sort of does, Rosie. Is the library free?"

"Yes. Kevin just finished his conference."

"Send her in and tell her I'll be there in a few minutes.

Offer her some coffee, and if she takes it, get me a cup too."
For the next few minutes he busied himself organizing the papers he'd been working on and rubber-banding them to the
file. Experience had taught him that failure to do so could result in mixed up files and billable time lost while straightening
up the mess.

When he entered the library, the young woman, dressed
in stone-washed jeans and a loose white blouse showing a
considerable amount of attractive cleavage, was seated at the
head of the table. "I see you're not a coffee drinker."

"I drink it, but the way I feel today it'd make me nervous."
Her statement was confirmed by the tightness of her face.

"What's the problem with your dad?"

"That the son of a bitch is alive?" she replied with a gri-
mace.

He studied one of the bookshelves that covered three of
the walls. "Ms. Keller, this is a law office, not Murder Incor-
porated. What has your father done?"

"He's abused my mother, my brothers and me all of our
lives. He used to come into the house drunk as a lord, yelling
and screaming. He'd beat us up, break dishes and furniture
and then expect to be treated like a loving husband and father."

Ian shook his head. "You told me about that at our first
meeting. What's he done *lately*?"

"Last night he slashed my tires."

"How do you know it was him?"

"I saw him *do* it."

"How come you didn't stop him?"

"Didn't have time."

"Tell me about it."

"I was in the kitchen, feeding Jimmy when I heard Jim shout. I rushed into the living room and saw someone messing with my car. He was bending over my right front tire. Then he stood up and I could see it was my father. He laughed, got into his car and drove off. When I got to my car all four tires were flat—slashed with a knife."

"Where was this?"

"Colden Avenue, at Jim's house. He's my boyfriend. I live there, Jimmy's our kid."

"What'd you do?"

"Called the police. They're looking for him."

"Any idea why he did it?"

"He's probably still pissed off over the last episode. He's gotta show up in court on Monday."

"Which was . . . ?"

"After my mom's funeral we were all at Carey's having dinner. That's where mom used to work as a waitress. As usual the old man was drunk. He started to talk about Mom. Something like 'the bitch took long enough to croak.' I told him to shut the fuck up. He stood up at the table, grabbed a serving dish of pasta, poured it all over me, and then smashed me over the head with it. I had to get two stitches." She pulled her hair back and pointed to a small white scar at the top of her forehead.

". . . Then what happened?"

"My brother Barry called 911. They sent an ambulance for me and the cops for him. He's out on bail for assault. The trial's Monday."

"Your father's a real nice guy. I'm glad he wasn't mine. . . . So what was it you wanted to see me about?"

She cleared her throat. "It's just . . . the three of us are having so much trouble with him, and we could really use some help."

Ian held up his hand. "Angela, I really feel for you and Barry, but there's a problem—there may be a conflict of interest. If I file objections to the will on behalf of Terry, I may need testimony to your mother's physical and mental condition at the time the will was signed. I may want to ask you, and maybe Barry, to testify. Under what's called the *Dead Man's Statute*, no interested party can testify about a transaction with the deceased. I assume you want what you believe to be the share in your mother's estate."

She nodded.

"Then you're an interested party."

She frowned. "But I won't be testifying about a transaction. I'll just tell about what she said and how she looked, and the like."

"That's a transaction. I think you and Barry had better get your own lawyer. Of course, to the extent it helps Terry, I'll work with him."

She shook her head. "I can't *afford* a lawyer."

He let out a breath. "I wish I could help."

CHAPTER 16

IAN RETURNED FROM COURT AT half past twelve thinking he'd have a whole afternoon to catch up on his paperwork. As he reached for his stack of mail and phone messages, Rosemary Lennon raised her head above her triple chins. "Where've you been, Mr. Elkins? They've been waiting over an hour."

"What? Who? I have no appointments for today."

"Mr. and Mrs. Linden. I called your cell a couple of times, but you didn't pick up."

He scratched his nose. "Sorry it happened again, but I was in the middle of trying the Jenkins dispossess."

She let out a breath. "Mr. Linden is quite annoyed at having been kept waiting."

He shrugged. "Where are they?"

"I gave them coffee and some of Mr. Rooney's donuts, and I put them in the library."

Ian hurried to his room, pulled the file, and rushed to the conference room. Barbara was seated on the left side of the table, sipping coffee; Roger, on his feet, looking as if engaged in an exercise walk, turned to face him in what appeared to be a modified shooter's stance.

"Where the fuck have you *been?* We've been cooling our heels for *hours*."

Ian knitted his brow. "I just got back from court. Did we have an appointment?"

Barbara was about to say something, but Roger cut her off with a glare. "Didn't the secretary call you and say we were waiting?"

"I was in the middle of trying a case and couldn't answer my cell. What's this about?"

Roger opened the button on his blue blazer, seated himself, and scratched the right side of his dark brush-mustache. "You're doing a crappy job on our case, and we're firing you."

Ian put the file on the table and turned to Barbara. "Are you here to discharge me as your attorney, Mrs. Linden?"

"That's what I told you, counselor," Roger declared, slowly enunciating each word.

"Excuse me, Mr. Linden," Ian replied, imitating the man's delivery. "*You* are not my client. *Mrs.* Linden is, and only she can discharge me." Linden looked daggers as Ian turned to face Barbara. "Are *you* discharging me, Mrs. Linden?"

Barbara looked uncomfortable, then set her jaw. "Will you excuse us for a few minutes, Ian?"

He nodded. "When you're ready for me, hit the intercom button and press seven." He pointed to the phone and departed.

In his office Ian opened one of the files he intended to work on, but the words jumped in and out of focus. He slammed it down on his desk. "That fucking sonofabitch.

Who needs him?" Ten minutes later the intercom buzzed. "Elkins."

"Mr. Elkins, this is Roger Linden. Can you come back in? We're ready to talk."

When he returned, Barbara was seated as before and Roger was seated on the opposite side of the table. Ian took a chair at the head of the table and tented his hands.

Barbara cleared her throat. "You are not discharged, Ian. Roger is a high-powered business executive, and he's accustomed to having his own way. He's really a very nice person. He didn't mean what he said."

She turned to her husband, who nodded. "Sorry, Ian. I lost my temper."

". . .No offense taken," Ian replied, wondering what the *quid pro quo* was.

"From here on," Barbara continued, "you are authorized to give my husband any information about the case he asks for."

"Does that include anyone *he* authorizes, including his company's counsel?"

She nodded.

"What about making decisions?" Ian asked, wondering whether he was pressing his luck.

She faced her husband, shook her head slightly, then returned her attention to Ian. "No. I've promised to consult with him, but the decisions will be mine."

"Your mother, your decisions," Roger said with a smile, then facing, Ian, "Fill me in."

"As you know, after a lot of prodding, they sent me an informal account, which I sent to Barbara."

"Yeah, and it showed half the six million we knew the old

lady had."

"You expected that, because Herb spoke to Barbara about joint accounts."

"She *never* gave him joint accounts," he nearly shouted.

"Please, Roger, you promised." Barbara was glaring at him across the table.

"Sorry. Continue, Counselor."

"I've been pressing Herb's lawyer to give us copies of all joint accounts and any documents, including powers of attorney, that were used to create them."

"And?"

Ian unsuccessfully attempted to stifle a chuckle.

"What's so funny?"

"Sorry. You sound just like my wife when she's leaning on me."

Roger laughed. "Does it work?"

"Damn straight. In any event, I've given him an ultimatum. Either I get the papers by a deadline, or we start a compulsory accounting."

"And when's the deadline."

"A week from Wednesday."

"And if he doesn't deliver, what will you do?"

"If Barbara authorizes the procedure and agrees to pay for it, I go ahead."

"And will you?" he asked, turning to Barbara.

She nodded.

THE FOLLOWING MONDAY WAS THE adjourned date for the Doyle estate. Ian was happy to be in surrogate's court instead of L&T. From a physical standpoint, the courtroom was large and bright, unlike the cramped rooms in the basement of the courthouse. More important were the atmosphere and the people: In surrogate's court, he knew nearly everyone. Surrogate Bill Anderson and Herb Crowley, his principal court attorney, were close personal friends. While he wasn't given unfair advantage over anyone, the interchange was always cordial, and he knew he would get the time and opportunity to represent his clients properly. Downstairs, the atmosphere was rushed. There were too many cases, too few judges, hearing officers, and clerks, and the pressure created by all that was, to say the least, uncomfortable.

When the case was called, Mike Bono answered ready.

"What's your position, Mr. Guardian Ad Litem?" the judge asked.

"I'd like a 1404 examination," Ian replied, referring to a statutory right to examine the witnesses to a will, and the attorney who drew it, before deciding whether to object to probate.

"If Your Honor please," said Bono, "he can't have a 1404. As Mr. Elkins knows, Edgar Cohan, the draftsman and one of the witnesses to the will, is dead, and Hal Morton, the other witness, can't be found."

The judge turned to Ian. "What do you say to that, Mr. Elkins?"

"I accept that Edgar Cohan can't testify, but his son Edgar, Jr. should be able to shed some light on the matter."

"You can subpoena him if you file objections," said Bono.

Ian shook his head. "There's more. The efforts that were made to locate Morton were pretty puny."

"Then you locate him if you can."

"That's your job, not mine, Mike."

"I'll take that under advisement," said the judge. "You

have anything else?"

Ian nodded. "Yes, Your Honor. I'd like to depose Barry Keller, Sr., the proponent of the will. Maybe he can tell us something."

"The rules don't permit that until objections are filed."

"I think we can waive that, Mr. Bono, considering there's no one else."

Bono's face reddened. "That'll be a problem, Judge. Mr. Keller's in jail for assault. *She* put him there." He pointed to Angela."

"Well, he beat me up."

"Who are you, young lady?"

"I'm Angela Keller, Judge. I'm Mary Doyle's daughter."

"Are you and your brother—" The judge looked down at the file—"Terrance the only children of Mary Doyle?"

"No, there's my brother Barry."

"Where's he?"

"He had to work. I'm here for the two of us."

"Does either of you have a lawyer."

"No, Judge. I asked Mr. Elkins to help me, but he said he has a conflict."

The judge scratched his chin. "He's probably right. I'm going to adjourn this case for two weeks. I strongly suggest you and your brother get a lawyer."

CHAPTER 17

SEVEN-TEN ON TUESDAY EVENING FOUND Ian trudging to the office door. He'd put in a long, hard day—in court 'til three- thirty and digging through a pile of paperwork since. He was bushed and looking forward to dinner and some time with Helen and Carol.

Just as he reached the door, the phone rang. He was tempted to let voice mail get it, but his work ethic overcame his common sense. "Rooney and Associates."

"And may I be speaking to Ian Elkins?"

"Barney?" He sounded just like Mark's brother-in-law.

"Who's Barney?"

"You're not Barney Moran?"

"Tim Kilcullen."

"Sorry, you—uh, you sound just like him. I'm Ian Elkins. How can I help you."

"I'm an old family friend of Mary Doyle and her children. Angela tells me you're a guardian for Terry, but you can't represent her or Barry."

"That's right. They need their own lawyer. Are you one?"

"I am that."

"Then we can work together to help all three of them. Do you do estates work?"

"No, but I'm the best damned trial lawyer you'll ever meet."

"Good. I can help with the surrogate's procedure, and you can work your magic on the judge or jury. The case is on in court a week from tomorrow. You can file a notice of appearance."

". . . There's a wee bit of a problem there."

"Oh?"

"I'm on a six-month suspension. Nothing serious, I just punched out a court clerk. I won't be able to appear for the kids for another three weeks—that's the end of the month. Can you put it over 'til then?"

"I'll try. In the meantime, I'll send you copies of all of the court papers."

As he walked to his car, Ian wondered what he should tell the judge. Maybe Herb Crowley could give him some advice.

EARLY THE NEXT AFTERNOON HE FOUND Herb in his office. The room reminded Ian of his own when he had been part of the law department. All the court attorneys had two windows, from the lowest beginner to the principal. Herb was on the phone at a desk perpendicular to the entrance. Ian removed the files from the emptiest of the visitors' chairs and seated himself. A few minutes later, Herb hung up and grabbed Ian in a bear hug. "Great *seeing* you! Where you want to eat?"

"You pick it. I've gotten into the lousy habit of eating

lunch at my desk or Mark's."

"That's one of the bad things about private practice. I did the same thing when I worked for my uncle. Judge McCann was right. A regular lunch with friends is good for the soul, and it produces better work."

Ian nodded, remembering the kindly surrogate he and Herb had worked for. "Where will it be?"

"I've been going to the Yankee Tavern lately."

"The bar?"

"Yeah, but they have good sandwiches, especially the wraps."

Ten minutes later they entered the tavern. At the corner of 161st Street and Gerrard Avenue, it was only two and a half blocks from the courthouse. The restaurant was still fairly crowded, and there were no tables for two available, so the they took adjoining seats at the 161st Street end of the long bar.

"I see you're right about this place for lunch," Ian said, noticing more than half of the bar patrons eating sandwiches or hot dishes along with their drinks, many of which were non- alcoholic.

"Stick with me, kid."

"I'll take you up on that. I could use a little sage advice."

"Ask away . . . though, when we were together in the court, I was usually the inquirer."

Ian told him about the call from Kilcullen.

"Interesting. . . . He really clobbered a clerk?"

Ian nodded.

"What's the problem?"

". . .I just think that bringing up the suspension in open court as a reason for another adjournment could be embarrassing to the two older kids, and I feel that my ward would do better if he was together with his siblings."

"You're right. You *do* need some sage advice."

Ian knitted his brow.

"You're too sensitive. If the judge asks why, just tell him. Bill's not going to hurt you or your kid. Besides, Mike has no right to use Kilcullen's suspension against any of the objectants. Just let it come out, and don't worry."

IN THE AFTERNOON A FEW days later, Kathy Rooney visited her brother in the federal lockup. It was a relatively pleasant visit and helped keep his spirits up. As she was about to leave the building, she was accosted by a tall, broad-shouldered man in a dark-blue suit with a shock of curly brown hair. "Mrs. Rooney?"

"Yes?"

"My name is Evan Kent. I'm with the U.S. Marshal's Service." He showed her his badge. "Could we talk for a few minutes?"

"Is it about Barney?"

"Yes, ma'am."

She nodded.

They took an elevator up to the next floor, where he led her to an unmarked door and into a small room. He seated himself behind a bare, green-topped steel desk, and she took one of the two visitor's chairs and crossed her left foot over the right. "Can I get you some coffee?"

She shook her head. "What about Barney?"

"The trial of his bosses comes up next week in the Bronx. The federal racketeering trial is scheduled for two weeks after that."

"Does Barney know that?"

"Not exactly. The DAs will tell him tomorrow."

She scratched her left knee through the gray wool slacks. "What are you trying to tell me?"

"You know the deal he made for his case?"

"He pleads guilty to a misdemeanor, he's sentenced to time served, and he goes into witness protection."

"That's right. I'm in charge of his witness protection team."

"Oh. . . . How can I help you?"

"First, I want to fill you in on what's going to happen." Kent opened a thin manila folder and took out a single sheet of paper. "After the federal trial, we'll drive him to Teterboro Airport and fly him by private jet to an airport in the Midwest. During the next few days we'll house him in a federal correctional facility, orient him, and give him his new identity documents. Then we'll drive him to his new home, and we'll help him to set up at home and at his job."

"And then?"

"We let him get on with his life."

". . . You're just going to *desert* him?"

"No, ma'am, we will be watching out for him. We'll make random visits. And he can always call us."

She breathed a sigh of relief. "What do you need from me?"

"We'd like you to pack his clothing and some domestic items so that he can have them at his new home."

"How can I send them to him? I'm not supposed to know where he'll be living."

"You won't know. There'll be a gradual pickup of packages that will be sent to a federal distribution point and secretly shipped to him"

"What about his furniture?"

He shook his head. "Too bulky. Taking it out will alert the bad guys. We'll buy him new stuff."

"...There is one other thing."   "Yes?" he said.

"I'm the trustee of a trust fund for his benefit. If I don't know where he is, how do I get payments to him?"

"You don't. Trying to could lead the mob to him."

She wrung her hands. "But he needs that money to *live* on. He's always been able to count on it. When he tried to make more, look what happened!"

The marshal shook his head. "He's just going to have to grow up and support himself."

CHAPTER 18

THAT RAINY FRIDAY HARLEY GOLDBERG met his client for lunch. The lawyer had been pressing for the sit-down for nearly two weeks and had finally overcome Herb's claims of being overworked during busy season by scheduling the meeting at a deli pizzeria only a block from the client's office. They were in the middle booth of the seven across from the pizza counter.

"Not bad," Harley commented of his ham, swiss, and pepper hero.

"I told you so. We order up from here almost every day." Herb bit into his second slice of pepperoni pizza.

"Funny how we Jews get together to break bread along with all the dietary rules."

Herb chuckled, then frowned.

"What's the matter? I say the wrong thing?"

"Look, Harley, I'm up to my ass in work right now. You told me we had to have this meeting. Let's get to it."

"Sorry," the lawyer replied, putting on his most contrite

face. "Your fucking sister's lawyer is pushing me to give him copies of all joint accounts, the powers you used, and everything else. If he doesn't get it, he's going for a compulsory accounting."

"So give them to him," Herb replied, glaring. "I told you that before. You have copies of everything."

"*Damn* it, Herb! That's not the way to do it." Harley slammed his sandwich down on the plate. "I've been trying to tell you that, but you won't listen. That's why I insisted on a face-to-face."

The accountant let out a breath. "Okay, I'm listening."

Harley lifted his sandwich and gestured with it. "In the first place, we all know that, as soon as I give him all the records, he'll demand that you put back all of the joint accounts, and that, if you don't he'll bring the compulsory."

"So? That sets us up for the settlement talks we want."

"Yeah—with you on the short end." Harley was about to pound the sandwich on his plate for emphasis but took a bite instead.

"Then what do we do?"

Harley finished his bite and wiped his lips with a finger. "I tell him to go to hell."

Herb picked up a slice then set it down. "Then he goes for the compulsory anyway."

The lawyer smiled broadly. "*Right.*" Herb looked puzzled. "That's what we *want* him to do. He brings the compulsory *without* the records."

"Won't the judge require us to give them to him?"

"Eventually, but while we're fighting about them, we're on even ground, and *that's* when the judge will start pushing us for a settlement."

Herb smiled. "Tell me, Harley, where can I buy brass balls like yours?"

THAT EVENING AT THE KAPLANS', dinner was nearly over. They'd stuffed themselves on Molly's chicken parmigiana and were just finishing generous helpings of cherry pie with vanilla ice cream. Sam patted his stomach. "Molly, that was a stupendous dinner."

She reveled in the compliment for a moment, wiped the smile off her face, and turned toward her husband. "I'm glad you liked it, dear, but I wish you'd eat a little less. I'd like to have you with me for more than just a little while. You know what the doctor said."

Sam shook his head. "Eh, what does he know? I'll be around to bother you for a long time. . . . And if not, you can get the sports model you always wanted."

Molly blushed.

"*Ma!*" Freddie Goldstein exclaimed. "Do I have to sit around in the living room again while everybody's yakking?"

Betty looked at her mother, who spread her palms. "What do you want to do?"

"Can I watch TV?"

"Go into Grandpa's den,"

"And take your cousin with you," Betty added.

"Do I *have* to?"

"Of course you do."

"But *Ma*, she's a baby. . . . Besides, she's a *girl.*"

"What's wrong with girls? Your mother was one, and so was your grandma."

"Oh, *okay,*" he grunted and waved at Carol. "Come on, kid."

Carol looked questioningly at her mother. "Go with your cousin. Show him that us girls are better than boys."

After the children left, the adults repaired to the living room. Once the coffee was served and Sam had gotten his usual brandy, he turned to his son-in-law. "So? What's exciting in the legal field?"

Molly glared at him. "Why don't you ask your partner what's new and exciting in accounting?"

Eric laughed. "That's easy, Mom. *Nothing.*"

Sam chuckled and turned to Ian. "Okay, *boychick, sing.*"

Ian smiled and shook his head. "Okay. Which story do you want? I work on a lot of cases."

"The one where the teen-aged boy is getting nothing from his mother's estate" Betty said.

"*Hey,*" Sam declared. "You're stepping on my territory. . . . But, okay, what's new in that case?"

"There *is* something. The older sister told me about a friend of her mother, woman who used to work with her at the restaurant, name of Gwen Collins. She told me that Gwen knows about the beatings her father gave Mary, and that the mother told her she was leaving everything to her children."

"Have you spoken to Gwen?" Helen asked.

"This afternoon. She's visiting her relatives in Ireland, and I just ran up Mark a big phone bill."

"What did she tell you?" Sam asked.

"Not as much as I'd like. She confirmed that she and Mary were friends and worked together. She did say that Mary would come to work with bruises, and sometimes a black eye."

"Did she say the father gave it to her?" was Eric's question.

"Hard to say. She did say Mary cried when she asked her what'd happened, and when she brought up Barry's name she'd nodded."

"Who's Barry?" Sam asked.

"The father. The older son is Barry, Jr."

"What about the will?" asked Betty. Did Mary tell her about what she was doing for her kids?"

"Again, sort of. She knows that Mary wanted everything to go to her children, and she once said she had taken care of them, but she refused to be specific."

Sam sipped his brandy. "What're you going to do?"

"I asked her if we could meet when she gets back from Ireland next month, and she said okay and gave me her address and phone number, but I have a feeling I'm not going to get much from her."

Helen looked puzzled.

"From what the daughter told me and what I could gather, I think she's scared to death of Barry."

CHAPTER 19

THE NIGHT AFTER THE BRONX TRIAL, Barney was back in his eight-by-ten single cell. He was grateful for the relatively generous size but wished he had someone to talk to. He realized, however, that solitary was for his protection. Seated on his suspended bunk, furnished with a thick pad for a mattress, he was picking at a dinner of boiled chicken, string beans, and mashed potatoes swimming in a white gravy, with a wedge of soggy apple pie and lukewarm coffee, on a steel tray on his lap. The food they served was high-calorie and might even have been wholesome, but it was far from appetizing, and he had lost over five pounds since his incarceration. He forced himself to eat a little more than half the meal, then pushed the tray under the bars. He picked up one of the magazines Kathy had brought and settled down on his bunk to read until lights out.

"Hey, Barney, you've got a visitor," announced the slightly overweight, middle-aged corrections officer who had *cafe au lait* skin and was in charge of Barney's section.

"Who is it, Smiddy—uh, I mean, Mr. Smith?" Barney mentally kicked himself for breaking that rule.

"It's your sister, Mrs. Rooney."

A burly young White officer joined Smith, and the two entered Barney's cell, cuffed his hands in front of him, put on leg irons, and led him out.

"You really don't have to do that," he protested. "I'm not going to run away."

"I know," Smith replied, "but rules are rules."

They led him to an elevator that took them down two levels and from there to a line of five booths. He took his seat in the middle one, and his leg irons were attached to the crosspiece of the chair. Kathy, her dark hair pulled back in a tight ponytail and wearing a smart camel-colored blazer, was seated opposite him separated by a sheet of bulletproof glass. Barney picked up his handset. "Hi, sis. You look great." He pointed to his own garish orange jump suit. "How've you been?"

"Just fine. How'd court go today?"

"Okay, I guess."

"What do you mean by that?"

He knitted his brow. "The direct testimony went just like me and the DA rehearsed it, and the cross wasn't bad. Tony's lawyer kept stressing how my indictment got lowered from a felony to a misdemeanor, but we expected that."

"Sounds like it went okay. What was wrong?"

"The way they *looked* at me. And every time Mario did he mouthed 'you're dead.'"

Kathy shivered. "I'm glad you're going to be in witness protection. . . . But I'll miss you."

". . .I'll miss you too, sis. But I guess it's gotta to be."

A tear ran down Kathy's cheek. "Does it really have to be

forever?"

He shook his head. "Not forever, but for a long time. The marshals told me that after, five years, it might be safe to work out some contact."

She scratched her chin. "That reminds me—I've packed up your clothes and some of your small items. They've been picking up packages every few days."

"Yeah, thanks. . . . There is something else."

"What?"

"The trust. They're getting me a job at a Wal-Mart, but it doesn't pay that much. I'm going to need money from the trust."

She shook her head. "They told me not to send you any. It'd be too dangerous."

He frowned. "They told me that, too . . . but how'm I gonna live?"

"Please, Barney. I'll give you some money to go away with, but after that I can't give you any more 'til it's safe."

He shook his head. "Look, Kathy, I know you want to keep me alive, but living on the salary of a Walmart clerk isn't living. Don't worry—I'll figure something out."

Kathy was in tears as they led Barney back to his cell.

ON THE FIRST MONDAY OF THE MONTH, Ian found himself in surrogate's court, waiting for the calendar to be called. He looked around the courtroom, hoping to find his new co-counsel. "Good morning, Ian," said Mike Bono, tugging at the points on his vest. "Where's your new Clarence Darrow?"

"I guess he'll be here. I spoke to him last night, but I don't know what he looks like."

"There's no notice of appearance on record."

"I guess he'll file one today. He only came off suspension yesterday."

"If you say so," Bono replied with a chuckle.

The courtroom door opened, and Angela came in with her kid brother in tow. The young man was wearing a sweatshirt with *SGHS* in bold black letters on the front.

"Morning, Terry," said Ian. "Shouldn't you be in school?"

"I wanted to see Uncle Timmy."

"I didn't know he was your uncle."

Angela smiled. "Tim's not a relative, but he's the closest thing any of us'll have to an uncle."

"What's that on your shirt?"

Terry looked down. "It's clean."

"I mean the letters."

Angela laughed. "That's his school. Samuel Gompers High School."

"Yeah, I'm going to be an auto mechanic," Terry added.

"Not if you keep cutting school," Ian replied.

Terry shrugged.

At that moment there was a loud bang, and the court clerk announced, "All rise. The Honorable William Anderson. Draw near, give your attention, and you will be heard."

The judge entered from a door on the right and climbed to the bench. "Be seated," said the clerk.

Bill Anderson finger-combed a shock of dark hair just beginning to gray, and smiled as he surveyed the crowd. "Good morning, ladies and gentlemen."

"Good morning, Your Honor," the chorus of lawyers replied.

"Mr. Greene, will you please call the calendar?"

Donald Greene smiled, mopped a bead of sweat from a

dark brow that contrasted with his stark, curly-white hair, and began to do so.

I'm going to miss that guy, Ian thought, remembering that Donald was retiring at the end of the year.

The probate calendar was called first. The Doyle Estate being number seven, was reached in less than five minutes, and Ian and Bono put their appearances on the record. "Who are you?" the judge asked, looking at Angela and Terry.

"I'm Angela Keller. I'm Mary Doyle's daughter. This is my brother, Terry."

"He's my ward, Your Honor," Ian added.

"Isn't there another child?" the judge asked, looking at the folder.

"My brother Barry had to work," she replied.

"Weren't you and Barry supposed to be getting a lawyer?"

"They're going to be represented by Timothy Kilcullen, Your Honor," said Ian.

"Where is he?" the judge asked.

"Right here, Your Honor," boomed a voice from the entrance door. Down the right side of the courtroom strode a man the very picture of a retired football player. He was six foot four, with broad shoulders, an expanding waistline, and the beginnings of a double chin, topped by a square beard and a shock of curly hair with salt-and-pepper coloring. He was dressed in a black suit decorated with silver threads, a gray shirt and, a flowered black tie. Upon reaching the counsel table, he put an arm around Angela and turned to the reporter. "Timothy Patrick Kilcullen, Your Honor. I appear for my godchildren Angela and Barry Keller."

"Have you filed a notice of appearance?" asked the judge.

"Not yet."

"Please do so promptly."

"I will."

"Will you be filing objections?"

"Mr.—" Kilcullen looked at a thin folder— "Elking—" he looked questioningly at the other two lawyers, and Ian nodded at him— "told me there were some witnesses to be examined first."

"Excuse me, Your Honor," said Mike Bono, "but Mr. Elkins knows he can't get a 1404 examination."

"Why not?" asked the judge, and noticing a puzzled look on Kilcullen's face, continued. "I see you're not familiar with surrogate's court practice. Section 1404 gives you the right to examine the attesting witnesses and the scrivener at the estate's expense before putting in objections." The judge then turned back to Bono. "Why not, Mike?"

"One of the witnesses to the will is dead, and the other can't be found."

"What about the scrivener?"

"He's the one who died, Your Honor."

The judge turned to Ian. "What about that, Mr. Elkins?"

"The scrivener's son is available. He can at least testify as to his father's signature, and I don't think Mr. Bono made a sufficient effort to locate the other witness."

"The affidavit of due diligence is in the file," Bono replied.

"But all you did is check the web. And what about your petitioner, Barry Keller, Sr.?"

"You can examine both of them if you file objections."

The judge let out a breath, then motioned to Herb Crowley. "Give me a memo on that, Mr. Crowley. We'll adjourn the case 'til a week from Wednesday, and I'll give you my ruling then. If either counsel wants to brief the issue, give it to

Mr. Crowley by Monday."

As they left the courtroom, Angela turned to Ian. "Have you spoken to Gwen Collins?"

"Not yet. She won't return my calls."

She turned to Kilcullen. "The old bastard got out of jail last week. I guess he scared her."

"I'll try to get in touch with her," he replied.

CHAPTER 20

A T 5:45 IN THE AFTERNOON OF a cold, dark, drizzly Tuesday, Ian, seated behind his messy desk, was dictating into a micro-cassette recorder when the intercom buzzed. "Yeah?"

"How's it going, kid?"

"Oh, it's you, Mark."

"Who'd you expect, the Lone Ranger?"

"I thought you'd be out all day."

"Just got back. We settled Bartolli just before the jury came in."

"How'd you make out?"

"Better than if we'd waited for a verdict. I collared a juror in the corridor. We were about to lose it five to one."

"Mario must've been happy."

"Overjoyed. He gave me a bottle of McCallan's twelve-year-old."

"Not in lieu of a fee, I hope?"

"Hell, no. I'm a lawyer, not a charity. Want a nip?"

"Love one."

"Bring in a tray of ice on your way."

"Will do. I'll be there in about ten minutes. I want to finish dictating the Harrison motion."

"That's the dismissal one?"

"Right."

Ten minutes later, Ian entered his boss's office with the ice and two glasses. Rooney had his jacket off and his feet resting on the writing pullout, and was poring through the day's mail.

They sipped their scotch in comfortable silence. After a while, Rooney spoke up. "It's so peaceful here, I almost hate to go home."

"Kathy mad at you?"

"Not this time." Rooney took a pull at his drink nearly emptying the glass. "I wish it were only that."

"Sounds serious. Any way I can help?"

The big man chuckled. "You're a good friend, kid. But you've already done all you can."

Ian looked puzzled.

"I didn't mean to keep you in the dark. It's about my fucking brother-in-law."

"He okay?"

"So far as I know. They finished the federal case a few days ago, and he went into witness protection."

"So what's the problem?"

"Nothing *I* can see, but Kathy's been moping around as if she were going to his wake." He finished his drink, poured a refill, and offered one to Ian, who declined.

Ian smiled. "Let me give you some world class Mark Rooney advice."

Rooney looked up and chuckled. "This'll be good."

Ian pointed a finger at his boss. "To quote the oracle, 'Ignore it. She'll get over it.'"

The big man laughed. "Now, you give me some *good* news."

Ian shook his head. "The best I can tell you is I'll be in court tomorrow on the compulsory for the Kronen estate."

"Great!" Rooney chortled. "Give'em *hell*."

WEDNESDAY WAS BRIGHT AND SUNNY. To Ian the improved weather portended good things. At the very least he wouldn't be stuck in L & T court. Having only one case seemed almost like a day off. He parked his ancient Volvo in the usual lot, picked up his attaché case with only one file in it, and walked the three blocks to the Bronx County Courthouse. Since it was a half hour before the calendar call, he first went to the court offices on the third floor and schmoozed with the various clerks. About a quarter after nine he ascended to the fourth floor and reached the courtroom just as Donald Greene, the court clerk, was unlocking the door. "Ian, good to see you," said the man in his clipped Jamaican accent.

"It's always great to see *you*. How's this court going to survive without you when you retire at the end of the year?"

The man smiled broadly. "I'll miss everybody, but the missus wants us to live with her family in the Islands. Can't take any more Bronx winters."

Ian spent the next fifteen minutes or so renewing old acquaintances. He looked forward to returning to the court and wondered whether Bill Anderson would be able to live up to his promise. He called out Harley Goldberg's name a few times hoping to meet the man before the calendar call, but got no response. He wondered what a Goldberg named after a motorcycle would look like. At last a gavel banged, and Donald Greene announced the entrance of the judge and the call of the calendar. Ian's case was near the end of it.

When it was called, a man of medium height and build, with straight blonde hair, and a thin blonde mustache dressed in a double-breasted brown suit, answered "Harley Goldberg for the respondent-executor."

"Are you consenting to a thirty-day order?" asked the judge—which required the account to be filed and moved for settlement within thirty days.

"May we have a conference, Your Honor?" Goldberg asked.

"Conference," said the judge, and nodded to the clerk to continue with the calendar.

A half hour later, when the call of the calendar was complete and the judge had repaired to his robing room to hold conferences, Ian sat down next to his adversary. "What's this about, Mr. Goldberg?"

"The *case*. What else, *Counselor*?"

"But what are you *looking* for in the conference?"

"You'll hear about it at the conference, *Counselor*."

Ian shrugged and drifted off: The man was a world-class snot.

Forty minutes later they entered the robing room behind the bench. The judge was in shirt sleeves, his tie loosened, his robe hanging on a coat tree. "Well, gentlemen, what can I do for you?" Ian was about to respond when the judge held up his hand. "I know what you want, Mr. Elkins. It's in your papers. What do *you* want, Mr. Goldberg?"

"Your Honor, there's no need for what Mr. Elkins is demanding. We've already given him an informal accounting. The only parties involved are a brother, a sister, and the sister's children. Surely they can resolve a family matter without the aid of the court."

The judge turned to Ian. "Did he give you an informal account?"

"Yes, Your Honor, but it showed only half the assets my client knows her mother had."

"The rest are in joint accounts that Mrs. Kronen created for her son's benefit. As Mr. Elkins well knows, they're not probate assets and aren't part of a probate accounting. I've given Mr. Elkins receipt and release forms, and if his client will sign them, she and her children will get what they're entitled to."

Ian reddened. "Judge, this is nonsense. I've asked Mr. Goldberg for copies of the records including the backup on when and how the joint accounts were created, including copies of any power of attorney that was used, but he's refused to give them to me. I need the judicial accounting in order to force him to give me those records."

"What about it, Mr. Goldberg?" the judge asked. "Give him the records he asked for, and I'll adjourn this case so you can resolve the estate without an accounting."

Harley put on his sweetest smile. "I'd like to, Your Honor, but my client is very annoyed that his dear sister doesn't trust him. Besides, he is a C.P.A.."

The judge glared at the lawyer. "Come off it, Mr. Goldberg. Neither Mr. Elkins nor I was born yesterday."

"Please, Judge," Harley replied, affecting a contrite expression. "I'll try to get my client to accede to Mr. Elkins's request. We'd really like to resolve this matter."

The judge shook his head and made a notation on the file. "Then you'd better do it quickly, because I'm granting the thirty-day order. Settle an order on him, Mr. Elkins."

CHAPTER 21

H OW IS IT?"

"Huh?" Ian asked looking up from his salad plate.

"I asked you *how it is.*" Helen was glaring at him.

"Yeah Daddy, do you like it?" asked Carol from her booster-seat at the glass-topped circular kitchen table that had replaced the breakfast bar.

"Sure," he mumbled absently.

"What is it you like?" Helen demanded.

He knit his brow for a few moments. "The table looks great," he said with a smile.

Helen shook her head. "We've had this table for nearly a month."

"Oh, Daddy," Carol sighed, mashed potato dribbling onto the bib that covered her pink jump suit.

"What's the matter, sweetheart?"

"Carol, you know what I told you about men?" Helen said, wiping a tear from her daughter's eyes.

"Yes, Mommy, they never notice anything."

"And what is your daddy?" She continued to hug the little girl.

"A man."

"Now tell him what he should have noticed."

"The salad." She grinned. "*I made it*. Did you like it?"

He took another mouthful and chewed slowly. "Very good. What's the flavor you put in the dressing?"

"Curry," Helen replied. "I got the recipe from one of her schoolmate's mothers."

An hour later, Carol had been put to bed, and Ian and Helen, were in the living room. "What's the matter? Something bothering you?"

"What makes you say that?" He picked up his coffee cup, then put it down.

She stared at him, suppressing a laugh. "You must be kidding. Look what happened at dinner."

"You know I don't notice things. As you told Carol, I'm just a man."

She nodded. "That's true, but there are limits. Something is bothering you. Is it the office?"

He shrugged. "What else?"

"There anything wrong?" she asked, concerned.

"Yeah, but it's nothing to bother you about."

"Don't give me that. If it's bothering you that much, I *should* know. Is it a client confidence?"

"No. Nothing like that. It's . . . Mark."

"*Mark*? Is he *sick*?"

He shook his head. "He's fine. It's Kathy and that idiot brother of hers. She's driving Mark nuts over him."

"I thought that problem was solved. He's in witness protection."

"Yeah, but she's been getting calls from his so-called friends, asking where he is."

"But she doesn't *know* where he is. . . . Does she?"

"No. And that's what she's telling them." He fiddled with a small stuffed bear Carol had left on the couch.

"Then what's the problem?"

He sipped some coffee. "For one thing, she thinks they don't believe her."

"Did anyone say something?"

"Sort of. You know—'He's your brother. How can't you know?' She tells them that that's the way the system works, that she can't know, but they tell her she's dead if they find out she's lying."

"Why doesn't she tell the authorities?"

"What's she going to tell them? They don't leave their *names*."

"That's terrible."

"It gets worse."

She knit her brow.

"A couple of days ago, she got a letter. It had no return address, but the postmark showed it had been mailed from Kansas City. It was from Barney. He asked her to call him next Sunday from a pay phone. The letter gave a phone number of another pay phone. It said he'd be needing money and wanted to work something out."

She gritted her teeth. "God what an idiot."

THE FOLLOWING WEDNESDAY, IAN WAS in court on the Mary Doyle Estate. "Well, gentlemen, is everybody ready?" the judge asked, smiling down on them.

All three lawyers had puzzled looks.

"Is there something the matter?" he asked with concern.

Ian spoke up. "The problem is, Your Honor, that when we were last before you, there was an issue of who Mr. Kilcullen and I could examine before we decided whether to object to the will. You told us to come back today for your decision."

Sheepishly, the judge looked in the file and read some papers. "Thank you for reminding me Mr. Elkins. We'll discuss that at a conference."

An hour later the three lawyers were seated before him in his robing room. "Can't this matter be resolved? The estate's not that large. Only a couple of houses worth a little more than half a million. You'll eat it all up in litigation."

"A half million in Bronx County is not that small, Judge." replied Mike Bono.

"That's true, Mike, but litigating the issue *could* eat a lot of it up." The judge looked down at the file. "Besides, they are your client's children."

Bono shook his head. "Judge, I'd like to help, but Barry Keller doesn't think they've been respectful to him."

"They'd've been a lot more respectful if the bastard treated them better," Kilcullen muttered, his face reddening.

The judge glared at Mike Bono, who cringed slightly. "Judge, I have tried, but all he says is, if they start behaving themselves, maybe he'll do something for them in his *will*."

The judge's expression softened. "Please try harder, Mike. I'm sure you have kids, too."

"I will, Judge," Bono replied, somewhat relieved.

"In any event," the judge continued, "we have several legal issues. The first question is who can be examined before objections are filed. Mr. Elkins wants to examine the proponent of the will and the son of the scrivener of the will."

Ian nodded.

The judge sighed. "Unfortunately, section 1404 doesn't permit it. The statute allows you to examine the witnesses and the scrivener, and, where the will has an *in terrorem* clause, the nominated executor and the proponent."

"A what?" Kilcullen asked.

"Judge, Mr. Kilcullen isn't an estates lawyer," Ian explained.

The judge looked at him. "Counselor, that's a clause that forfeits the bequest or inheritance of anyone who contests the will. This will does not have one. The only person you can examine before deciding whether to object is the other witness to the will—if he can be found."

Ian's expression darkened.

"However," the judge continued looking at Bono, "Mr. Elkins makes a point that your efforts to locate Hal Morton, the other witness, were perfunctory."

"Judge, we did an internet search. What else could we do?"

"How about hiring an investigator?" Kilcullen suggested.

The judge nodded.

"For this small an estate?" Bono's face was flushed.

"Excuse me, Your Honor," Ian interjected, "but wasn't Mr. Bono just telling us that a half-million-dollar estate in Bronx County *wasn't* that small?"

The judge smiled. "That's my recollection, too . . . Mr. Bono, I'm directing you to make a thorough search for Hal Morton and to report what was done, and the results, to the court. How much time will you need?"

"B-But, Judge, that's *wrong*."

"If you disagree with my decision, give me a memorandum of law. How much time will you need?"

"I'll try to get you something in two weeks."

"Serve copies on your adversaries."

The lawyer nodded.

"Adjourned for two weeks. Please call in the next conference."

As Ian walked out of the robing room, Kilcullen pulled him aside. "First time I've been in this fancy court. I could use some definitions."

"Fire away."

"What's a scrivener?"

"The lawyer who wrote the will."

"Who's the proponent?"

"The executor who wants it probated. Barry Keller."

Kilcullen smiled. "Now that I know it all, I'll win this case."

CHAPTER 22

ERB'S RELATIONSHIP WITH SALLY WAS the most exciting thing in his dull accountant's life, but even that had become somewhat predictable. On Friday nights they went out for dinner. That Friday he introduced her to Louie's, a restaurant in Port Washington, Long Island, where his parents had taken him when they wanted good seafood. It had been many years since he'd been there, not since his father died. Cora wouldn't go to Louie's or to any other restaurant she'd been to with her husband.

It was just as he remembered it—two large unpretentious rooms overlooking the sound, and the quality of the food had remained superb. They started with a dozen little necks. Then Sally a three-and-a-half-pound lobster with fries and slaw, while Herb ate sea scallops, one of his favorites. For dessert they split a banana cream pie with their coffee. It was a good thing that Sally had eaten well. She'd had a Manhattan while waiting for him to pick her up, and two more in the restaurant, and had drunk most of the bottle of chardonnay they'd ordered, and a brandy in her coffee.

She slept for most of the drive back to her apartment, and Herb assumed that he'd be putting her to bed and returning home without their Friday night sex. She surprised him. On their walk from the car to her apartment she leaned heavily on him, but when he tried to lay her down on the bed she pushed him onto it, ordered him to strip, and went to the bathroom to insert her diaphragm. This was followed by a two-climax coupling after which she fell asleep with him inside her.

HE AWOKE ON SATURDAY MORNING ON his back, with an erection brought on by her oral ministrations, at which point, she climbed aboard and pumped till they had reached a third orgasm. At nine, they shared a long, hot shower, and he put the coffee on while she made herself up.

At nine forty-five they went out and breakfasted at a coffee shop on Queens Boulevard. Sally consumed three fried eggs, a stack of pancakes, bacon, home fries, and buttered toast; he had two poached eggs and a slice of dry rye toast. As always, he wondered how she stayed slim.

As they were drinking their second cup of coffee he noticed her eyes riveted on him. "What's up?" he asked.

"What's bothering you?"

"Huh? . . . What makes you say that?"

"Cut the crap. It's obvious."

He wrinkled his brow.

"This morning before we got into the shower—you were looking out into space."

"I was just looking at the new print you got," he replied,

referring to a Chagall reproduction on the wall on the right side of her bed.

"Bullshit. When I'm on top, you always look at me. You love to look at my tits. It turns you on."

He hesitated. "Well . . . I was thinking about something."

She shook her head. "Tell Mama."

"The goddamned estate. How can I settle with my sister, with Roger egging her on?"

She signaled the waiter for a third cup of coffee and was halfway through it before she replied.

ON MONDAY EVENING, BARBARA HAD just finished cooking dinner when Roger got home. As he entered the kitchen, she ran up and hugged and kissed him endearingly. "Happy birthday, darling. How's my big boy?"

He laughed. "Not too bad for an old man."

"You'll never be an old man to me."

"Can I get you a drink?"

"White wine would be nice."

He went to the bar and brought back the wine and a scotch on the rocks for himself.

"How was your day?" she asked.

"Great. The guys took me out for lunch."

"That's nice."

"Funny thing happened when we got back."

"Oh?"

"There was a package waiting for me—a bottle of twenty-five-year-old Glenfiddich with a birthday card."

"Who from?"

"That's what was so funny," he said. "Your fucking brother."

IT WAS EARLY SUNDAY AFTERNOON by the time the Rooneys returned from the diner, where they'd had lunch with Bob and Anne Lutz, good friends and next-door neighbors. They'd met the Lutzs when they moved to Hartsdale, and went to mass together nearly every Sunday. While neither Bob nor Mark were big on religion, their wives were, and at their insistence the men had become regular, if not enthusiastic, Christians. Besides, the comradeship was pleasant—especially the food. Both men were world-class trenchermen, and seeing them from the waist down they could be taken for identical twins. That Sunday they had tucked into waffles drenched in butter and syrup with sides of Virginia ham while the ladies, for dietary reasons, limited themselves to poached eggs on English muffins.

Rooney invited the Lutzs in to see the Knicks lose another game on their new plasma TV, but Bob and Anne had to visit their grandchildren, so Mark took a beer, filled a bowl with chips, and settled down in his recliner to watch alone. Kathy was no sports fan; besides, she had to go out on an errand.

Forty minutes later, the Knicks had a slight lead and Mark was on his second Coors Light and third bowl of chips when he heard the front door bang shut. "Hi, honey," he said, but there was no response.

At half-time he had to empty his bladder and decided to use the master bathroom upstairs. When he got there Kathy was lying on top of their light-green checkered bedspread sobbing hysterically. "What *is* it?" he asked, gathering her into his arms.

Tears continued to flow for the next five minutes, and Mark began to wonder if he'd have to change his shirt. Finally, she pushed him off and sat up. "It's Barney," she rasped. "I don't know how he can do it."

"Do what?"

She shook her head. "He needs money."

"Where have I heard that before?"

"No, he really needs it. He can't live on what they pay him."

"Or won't. Let him tough it out. He's got to grow up."

She blew her nose. "It's worse than that. He borrowed money from the store."

Mark knit his brow. "You can't borrow money from a big chain store."

"They didn't know it. He sold some merchandise from the stock room."

"And?"

". . .They took an inventory and found the shortage."

"And he's not in jail?"

"He borrowed some money to pay them back."

Mark shook his head. "Let *him* pay back the loan."

"He can't. It's too much."

"How much?"

"He needs $3,500.00 by Wednesday."

"How much did he steal?"

"A thousand dollars' worth, but he borrowed fifteen hundred."

"Who from?"

She exhaled forcefully. "You know who. . . . The same kind of people he worked for in the Bronx."

"How'd you find out?"

"He just told me."

"You have his *phone* number?"

"No, I called a pay phone in Kansas City."

"From here?"

She shook her head. "I called from the phone booth opposite the post office. . . . I'll have to wire the money to him on Monday. Otherwise, they're going to do something bad to him."

Mark clenched his teeth. "I guess you have to. . . . But we've got to stop this."

"*How?*" she screamed as the tears began to flow again.

CHAPTER 23

TIM KILCULLEN DROVE HIS SILVER Caddy to the Kingsbridge section of the Bronx the next Monday night. The cold rain, a little more than a drizzle, was causing his windshield to fog. He had to use both the defroster and the air conditioner to keep it clear. He was tired and grumpy from a long day in criminal court, and he didn't relish the prospect of an evening out. He would much rather have been at Skelly's, his local pub, downing a few brews and bullshitting with the guys—but these kids were his godchildren. If only the bitch would respond to his letters or returned his calls— she could be an ideal witness. She'd worked with Mary for years, seen her come to work with a black eye, a split lip, or worse. She could testify how scared Mary was of Barry Keller, how she'd loved her kids and wanted to leave them everything but had been deathly afraid of him.

He turned onto West 132nd Street and drove until he lucked into a parking space just two blocks from his destination. The spot was tight, though, and took seven moves to get into. Maybe he should consider getting a smaller car. He climbed out, grabbed a slim folder with a legal pad and his umbrella, locked up, and trudged the short distance to a two-family house. There were two bells at the front door. Neither had a name. He assumed 972 A was for the upstairs apartment. He pressed the top button. After half a minute, getting no response, he rang a second time. Again no response. He tried a third time. Pressing his ear against the door, he heard a low buzz. When this didn't invoke a response, he held the button down for a full minute, then pounded on the door with the heels of his hands. Finally he heard a window open, and a deep male voice shouted, "What do you want?"

"Is Gwen Collins there?"

"Who wants to know?"

"Is she there?"

"Who the fuck are you?"

"Tim Kilcullen. I've got to talk to her."

"Get the hell out of here." The window slammed shut.

Tim pushed the button again and held it for a full two minutes.

Finally the window opened again. "Get the hell out of here. Stop bothering my wife."

Tim's face turned red. "I've got to talk to her. It's very important. . . . I'll keep ringing and banging 'til I do."

The window closed, and a minute later, through one of the side lights, Tim saw a light at the top of a staircase and a shape descending down the stairs. A moment later the door was opened by a broad-shouldered man half a head taller than Tim. "I told you to get the hell *out* of here," he said, reaching for Tim's collar.

AT ONE-THIRTY ON TUESDAY, IAN returned from court. He found an envelope waiting for him from Mike Bono—a report by an investigator of the further efforts to find the missing witness. The man had mostly repeated what Mike had done, made a trip to the address of the real estate office where the will was alleged to have been signed, but it was now a superette. There hadn't even been a Social Security search, though he assumed Mike would argue he didn't know the man's number.

He wanted to get Tim's take on it. The man was supposed to call him. He pressed the intercom. "Did I get a call from Mr. Kilcullen?" he asked.

Rosemary Lennon straightened her blonde hairpiece. "No, sir. If you'd had, you'd have gotten a message slip."

Ian phoned him, but got an answering service and left a message. He made several more calls during the afternoon, with the same result. At six, as the last one left in the office, he was about to leave when the phone rang. "Rooney and Associates."

"Ian, I'm glad I caught you."

"Tim! I'm glad, too. I was ready to leave. . . though I would've left the cell on. Have you read the report?"

"I haven't been in my office. . . . Something came up. You're going to have to adjourn the case tomorrow."

"Huh?"

Tim filled him in on his Monday night adventure.

"Gee, I'm sorry you weren't able to talk to her. What's that have to do with tomorrow."

"I'm representing myself in criminal court tomorrow. I broke the bastard's jaw, and the bitch filed criminal assault charges against me."

WHEN IAN RETURNED FROM COURT the next afternoon there six phone messages waiting for him, five from Roger Linden. "That man is impossible," complained Rosemary Lennon "On the last call he accused me of hiding you. He used terrible language and shouted that you weren't doing your job and should be fired. I put him through to Mr. Rooney. He wants to see you before you have lunch."

Ian found Rooney stuffing peanuts into his mouth while poring over a file. "Hi, Mark. I hear you were exposed to Roger Linden."

"A *real* pompous bastard," the big man replied with a shrug. "I suggested he shove the file up his ass.

Ian chuckled. "He can't fire us. His wife's the client, and she thinks I'm doing a great job."

"What *is* up with Kronen?"

"We've got a thirty-day order. It expires on Friday. He has thirty days to file an account and move it for judicial settlement," Ian continued, noticing his boss's puzzled expression.

Rooney brightened. "I assume you've gotten no papers. . . or a request for more time?" He pushed the can of nuts toward Ian, who shook his head.

"No on both counts."

"Would you give him more time if he asks?"

"Only if he gives me the paperwork I asked for."

"What do you propose doing after Friday?"

"I'll make a motion to remove him as executor and charge him personally for the legals."

"What about taking away his commissions?"

"His mother did that to him already. It's in the will."

"Sounds like you have it under control. Have fun."

"By the way you ought to have that fixed," Ian said pointing at two slats of the venetian blind on the far window that were hanging down at an acute angle.

"Yeah, Rosie had someone in to fix it, but the guy said it'd have to be replaced. I'll have a new one by next week."

IN HIS OFFICE, IAN OPENED the file and phoned Roger Linden. The man was out to lunch. At 4:00 he went back to the courthouse to file papers that were due that day. When he finished at 4:30, realizing that he had an appointment to meet with the director of his mother's nursing home, he went straight to his car where he phoned the office on his cell and learned that Roger had returned his call. Deciding that discretion was the greater part of valor he called Roger from the car. "Who the hell do you think you are, Elkins?" he shouted.

"Your wife's lawyer."

"Not for long. I'm firing you."

Ian restrained a chuckle. The man was laughable. It was the same crap he'd pulled a few months before. "Roger, I don't think you understand the ground rules."

"*What?*" The volume rose by several decibels. "How *dare* you?"

"How dare I what?"

"How dare you talk to a client like that?"

"In the first place, as you've been told before, you are not the client. Barbara is. You are entitled to any information you ask for, but she makes the decisions. . . . And furthermore, I don't appreciate your swearing at my staff."

"I *had* to. She was *hiding* you." The volume had gone down considerably.

"I was in *court*. I returned your five calls as soon as I got back." Ian wondered if Linden was going to bring up Mark's suggestion.

"Okay. What's up with the case?"

Ian filled him in, and the call terminated on nearly cordial terms.

ON FRIDAY A WEEK LATER, Harley Goldberg returned from lunch to learn he'd had a call from Herb Kronen. As he waited for the receptionist to place the return call he gazed at the long wall in front of his desk. It contained only diplomas. Maybe he should put up some prints, as Sally had suggested. He was taken out of his reverie by the buzz of the phone. "Hey, Herb, how're you doing?"

"I was fine 'til I got that package from you."

"What's the problem?"

"My sister wants to remove me as executor and charge me with the legals."

"That's not nice of her," Harley replied, suppressing a laugh.

"Didn't you file the accounting papers I signed for you?"

"Herb, this isn't the right time."

"Not the right time? When will the right time *be*? When the judge *removes* me?"

"Of course not. This is part of my tactic to get the settlement working. When the motion comes on, we'll have a conference. I'll promise to give him the papers he wants. Then we'll adjourn the motion and I'll give him some, but not all. We'll have another conference and I'll give him some more, and by the time their lawyer is worn down and your sister is getting sick of paying his legals, we'll work out a *good* settlement."

"I don't like it. It makes me nervous."

"Stop worrying, Herb. It'll work. I'm carrying the ball. I've done this before."

When he had finished the call, Harley made another one. "Hey, Sally, how's it going?"

"Great. What's up?"

"Our boy just got the papers. He's scared."

"That's what we expected. What can I do?"

"What you do best. That should calm him down."

Sally smiled and squeezed her thighs together as she put down the phone. It was going to be fun.

CHAPTER 24

THE FOLLOWING WEDNESDAY THE DOYLE Estate was back in court. Kilcullen and Ian had conferred over the telephone the night before. The investigator's report on his search for the missing witness was, they'd agreed, not overwhelming, but they were afraid it might pass muster with the judge.

When the case was called the judge set it down for a conference, and nearly an hour later, the three lawyers again entered the judge's robing room. "That new, Your Honor?" Ian asked, pointing to a coffee maker on a lower shelf of the bookcase at the rear of the judge's desk.

"Yes, Mr. Elkins, I decided make my own rather than send someone down every half hour to fill my cup. You, of all people, should be aware of my caffeine addiction."

"I remember it well," Ian replied with a smile, recalling the many times he had gone into Bill Anderson's office for a wakeup cup when he worked for him at the court. "It's a little small, isn't it?"

"We got it as a gift for opening a bank account, and my wife decided we really didn't need a four-cupper at home, but she's too frugal to throw it away."

"Saves the taxpayers some money," Mike Bono added.

The judge nodded. "So, Mr. Kilcullen, I hear you had an exciting evening last week."

Tim blushed and fingered the lapel of his electric blue suit. "So it would seem, Your Honor. I was trying to gather evidence for this very case when I was forced to defend myself."

"I understand the man was considerably bigger than you. How did you manage to disable him?"

"When I was a boy, I was in the toughest parochial school in the Bronx. You had to learn to fight or lose your lunch money. Later on I did some CYO boxing, and I once went up a few rounds in the Golden Gloves."

"I hear the other party filed criminal charges."

Tim nodded.

"How's that going?"

"Not too badly. I filed assault charges against him. . . . He did *start* the fight."

Anderson rubbed his chin. "Good move. In all likelihood they'll throw out both sets of charges when it comes to trial."

"That was my thought too, Judge."

"But," Anderson continued, shaking a finger, "I'll stand for no fighting in my court."

"I wouldn't think of it."

Ian looked at his co-counsel and wondered how a trial lawyer dared to wear such a flamboyant color in court. He and Mike Bono were both dressed in conservative suits, Ian's blue serge while Mike's gray flannel. The judge's jacket, which was hanging on the coat tree, was a low-key medium brown.

Anderson reached into the light-tan folder on his desk, pulled out the investigator's report, and skimmed it. "So where do we stand on the missing witness?"

"We tried to find him, Your Honor," Mike Bono replied with a forced smile. "Hired an investigator just like you told me to do."

"He didn't try very hard, Mike." said Ian. "He just redid your web searches."

"He went down to the office where the will was signed. As you can see, it doesn't exist any more."

"Big deal," said Kilcullen. "He made no efforts to trace where the real estate office had moved."

"What about the State Department?" Ian added. "Brokers and salesmen are licensed. . . . And, come to think of it, I don't see a Social Security search."

The judge held up his hand and re-read both the original and supplemental search. "Your adversaries do make a point, Mr. Bono. At the very least you should make license and Social Security searches."

"But, Judge, I don't have the man's Social Security number."

"I'll bet the Department of State has it," Ian remarked. "And maybe the son of the scrivener has some information on it."

"Judge, I'll try some more," Bono replied with an uncomfortable expression. "But it's not fair to hold up this estate indefinitely."

The judge blew out a breath. "I think you've all made good points. It's obvious that there is no one who can be examined under section 1404, and we can't hold up this estate indefinitely. Mr. Elkins and Mr. Kilcullen, you have one week to file your objections."

"But, Judge, we're entitled to examine *all* witnesses to the will before having to object," said Ian.

The judge shook his head. "If the man turns up, you can examine him. So file your objections. You haven't waived any rights with respect to the efforts made to find him." The judge turned to Bono. "And you are ordered to make a more extensive search for the witness, which must include at least searches in the Department of State and Social Security."

"But what about the number? I may not be able to get it."

"Then try a name search."

As the lawyers walked out of the robing room, Kilcullen laid a hand on Bono's shoulder. "Mike, they *are* his kids. Get us some money and stop all this crap."

Bono shook his head. "Believe me, I've tried."

THAT EVENING IAN RETURNED TO a noisy home. "I don't want him! Don't make me, Mommy!" Carol was screaming at a decibel level almost painful to Ian's ears.

He dropped his coat and attache case and rushed into the kitchen to find his princess crying hysterically. Her soft blonde curls were damp from her tears. "What's the matter, sweetie?"

She rushed to him and wrapped her arms around his legs. "Tell mommy *not* to. I don't *want* him!"

Helen turned from the stew pot on the stove and glared at him. "She's been going on like this for an hour. Don't you dare make me the villain."

He looked up at Helen in utter confusion. "What this is *about*?"

Helen looked down at her daughter. "Do you want to tell

your daddy, or shall I?"

"Don't let her *do* it, Daddy. Don't let her *do* it."

"Don't let your mother do what?"

"I don't *want* him."

"You don't want *who*?"

"A *brother*. Don't let Mommy get me one."

"I think maybe Mommy had better tell me about this." He looked up at Helen.

"Okay, Mr. Lawyer, let's see you solve this one. About an hour ago Carol pointed to my belly and asked me when her sister would come out."

"That sounds like a reasonable question. What did you tell her?"

"I said the baby would come out in about a month."

He nodded. "Yeah, it is getting close. Then what?"

"She asked what her sister's name would be,"

". . .And?"

"I told her, if it's a girl, we were going to name her Hannah, after my grandmother, and that if it's a boy, he would be Jack, after your dad."

"*No want Jack*!" The flow of tears turned into a river.

Ian choked back a laugh. "Why not?"

"No want 'nother *Freddie*!" She stamped her foot.

Ian tried to embrace her again, but she pushed him off. He thought for a moment, wondering what tack would work. "Your cousin Freddie's not *that* bad. It's just that he doesn't understand girls."

"Yes, dear," Helen added. "Most boys his age go through a time when they don't like girls. He'll grow out of it when he gets a little older. And when you get older, you'll get to like boys, too. *Especially* boys like your father."

Ian smiled. "Look, sweetheart, your mommy has no control over whether you'll have a brother or a sister. If it's Jack, he'll be named after your grandfather, who was a very nice man. Just like Grandpa Sam. You like him, don't you?"

"I *love* Grandpa. Promise, if it's Jack, he'll be just like Grandpa."

Ian hesitated, tempted to tell the absolute truth, but decided against it. "Yes, dear, just like Grandpa Sam." It worked; the little girl slowly calmed down.

When they'd put her to bed after supper, Helen turned to him and drily remarked, "You lawyers sure know how to lie."

He blushed, then smiled. "It would be more convenient if she were Hannah."

She looked puzzled.

"We'll be able to keep this apartment a while longer with two of the same sex."

Helen shook her head. "I've been meaning to talk to you about that. We're getting awfully cramped in here."

CHAPTER 25

IAN ENJOYED THE BRIGHT SUNNY weather as he drove his ancient Volvo to his regular parking lot before going to court for the return date of his motion to remove Herb Kronen as executor and charge him for the legals. He should have been in a great mood. He hadn't received answering papers from the other side, and, theoretically, the judge could grant the motion on default, but he knew better and was nervous, wondering what stunt Goldberg would pull.

He got there at nine, nearly a half hour before the calendar call, and went immediately to the accounting department. "How's it going, Sid?" he asked the nearly emaciated clerk who'd been the head of the department for over twenty-five years and was due to retire in December.

"Not too bad, Ian," the man replied, rising from his desk that backed on a window, and rubbing his cheek next to the gray beard that nearly matched his complexion. "But I'll be a lot better when I can get out of this place."

"Aw, come on. How's the Bronx County Surrogate's

Court going to survive without the expertise and dedication of Sidney Finkel?"

"They're going to have to, cause I'm not staying one minute past New Year's Eve," the other replied, leaning on the counter. "In the meantime, what can I do for you, or is this just a social visit?"

"Caught again. I did have a small inquiry. Anything filed in the Kronen Estate?" Ian gave the man a slip with the file number.

Finkel consulted a bound docket book. "There's your motion on for today, but other than that, nothing's come in for several weeks."

"Thanks, Sid. I didn't think there would be. See you around." As Ian headed off for the fourth floor, he wondered what Sid would do when he retired. He was a strange duck, a lawyer who had never practiced but always worked in the court system. Be an asset to any firm's estates department, but who would hire him?

The courtroom door was being unlocked. After making the rounds of his cronies, Ian took a seat in the left side of the first row to wait for the calendar call. A few minutes later he saw Harley Goldberg enter the room, wearing the same double- breasted brown suit he had the last time; Ian wonder if that was his only court outfit. Instead of coming over to greet him, Goldberg seated himself on the right side of the second row, and Ian resisted the impulse to go over and say hello.

At 9:35 Donald Greene banged a gavel on his desk to the right of the bench and announced the arrival of the judge.

When the case was called, Ian answered ready and the judge turned to Goldberg.

"I'll need a few more weeks, Judge."

Bill Andrews wrinkled his brow. The usual form of address was *Your Honor*, "Mark it for an application," he told the clerk.

There was a short recess before the judge heard the applications. "Ready to settle, Elkins?" Goldberg asked when Ian came over to try to learn what was going on.

Ian gritted his teeth. "I'm ready to take your default and try to work things out with your client's successor. . . who may very well be my client."

"Very funny," Goldberg replied and turned his eyes back to his *Times*.

Ian shrugged and returned to his seat. Fifteen minutes later the application was called and the lawyers again stepped up to the counsel tables. "Your honor," Goldberg began, "we'll need about three weeks."

Ian was about to respond but the judge held up his hand. "What for?"

"To answer the motion. This man wants to remove my client as executor from his mother's estate and charge him for the legals."

"If Your Honor please," Ian began, but the judge cut him off.

"I'm fully familiar with this matter, Mr. Elkins." The judge turned to Goldberg. "Counsel, your client was given thirty days to file his account and move it for judicial settlement. When he didn't comply with the order, Mr. Elkins moved to remove him and charge him with the legal expense. That gave you another three weeks. Have you filed the account and the proceeding?"

"Not yet, Your Honor, but—"

"When *did* you intend to obey the court's order?"

"I thought it would be better if you could resolve the matter. It's a family matter between a brother and sister." The lawyer looked shaken.

The judge turned to Ian. "Does your client want to settle?"

"We might, Your Honor, but not until we're served with a filed accounting and all of the records. As I previously advised Your Honor, we need all the documents relating to the joint accounts."

"I think your client has been very well advised by you," the judge said. He turned to Goldberg. "I will adjourn this motion for two weeks. If the account is not filed and moved for judicial settlement by then, you will get no more time."

"What about the records?" Ian asked.

"I'd like to add that, but I have no authority to order it until the account is filed and moved for settlement."

When Ian left the court room he was in his usual quandary. He'd achieved the best result possible, but Roger Linden would be on his head anyway over the delay.

"AW, COME ON, CARMINE. I just need a little more time." Sweat was standing out on Barney Moran's brow as he stood in front of a rectangular desk in what had been built as the first- floor bedroom of a six-bedroom colonial in the suburbs of Kansas City. Usually Carmine DiCaprio invited Barney to join him for an espresso, but this time the heavy-set man with the graying mustache, sitting behind the desk, had offered no such invitation. Barney had been awakened at 8:30 on a Sunday morning by Rocco, the man's driver and bodyguard, and practically dragged to the meeting.

"Look, Flynn, you owe me big, and you're way behind."

That made Barney even more nervous. Usually the man called him Joe, and one time even Mr. Flynn. "Please, Carmine, I'm good for it. I'll have it in just a little while." He wished he could sit down. The sun pouring through the high window behind the man's desk was making him squint.

The six-foot four-inch Rocco had been standing at attention next to his boss's desk. At a nod from the man he stepped forward and grabbed Barney by the collar. "That's *Mr.* DiCaprio," he hissed.

"Y-yes, Mr. DiCaprio."

Rocco released his grip, straightened his black suit jacket, and returned to his post.

"When's a little while?"

Barney fought to control himself and not piss in his pants. "Two weeks. I'm sh-sure I can have it by then."

DiCaprio shook his head. "Two weeks? No way. You'll bring it here by this Thursday. . . . By five in the afternoon."

Barney shuddered. "But, Mr. DiCaprio, that's too soon. It'll take more time."

"It better not. You know what happens to people who don't pay on time?" He pointed at Rocco.

"Want I should show him, boss?"

Barney glanced at the hulking shoulders and almost fainted.

DiCaprio knit his brows. "Not now. I think he knows." The man turned back to Barney. "You'd *better* know. . . . Now get the fuck out of here." He turned back to Rocco. "Show the bum out."

"I drive him home, Mr. DiCaprio?"

"Nah," said the man, showing off his teeth. "He can walk

or take a bus."

As Barney was half led and half dragged out of the house, he wondered if he had enough money with him for the bus.

Rocco shut the front door. The intercom rang. "Yes, boss."

"Watch and make sure he's gone. Then bring me an espresso, and one for yourself, too."

Ten minutes later Rocco returned and placed a tray with the two coffees and a plate of biscotti on his boss's desk, and was motioned to one of the visitor's chairs. Carmine took a sip and sighed. "This is what life's about."

The two sat in companionable silence for a while, drinking and munching. Then DiCaprio spoke up. "What you think about that dumb mick?"

"He's dumb alright."

"Something about him bothers me."

Rocco looked puzzled.

"He suddenly shows up in the neighborhood, knows how to find us. . . . I wonder. We got a picture of him?"

Rocco nodded. "Yeah, we got a couple with the loan apps."

DiCaprio scratched his neck. "Have a bunch of copies made up. Let's send them around. Who knows what'll turn up?"

CHAPTER 26

BOWING TO THE INEVITABLE, IAN and Tim Kilcullen filed their objections in the Doyle estate. Ian would have preferred to first examine Barry Keller, the petitioner and father of his ward, but this couldn't be, since he hadn't quite finished his short jail term for slashing Angela's tires. Deciding not to delay the estate, Ian noticed the deposition of Edgar Cohan, Jr. and had subpoenas served on him. A few days later, he learned there was a message that Mr. Cohan had called him, and he returned the call. "Ian Elkins, Mr. Cohan. Thanks for returning the call."

"You're welcome, and please call me Ed."

"Sure thing, Ed. I'm Ian."

"I got your subpoenas. What's this all about?"

Ian looked at a copy of an affidavit from Cohan in the court file. Doesn't know what it's about? he thought. The man must be kidding. "I'm a guardian ad litem for Terry Doyle in connection with the probate of what's claimed to be his mother's will. The will leaves everything to Barry Keller, my ward's father, and nothing to any of her children. The children have objected to the will."

"I know about that. My late father drew the will and was one of the witnesses. I gave an affidavit about that to Mike Bono."

Ian stretched his neck and noticed that his law school diploma was hanging at a rakish angle. He'd have to straighten it. "Your affidavit is part of the court file. You identified your father's signature on the will."

"Right. What do you think I can do for your case?"

Ian scratched his chin, wondering if the guy could, or would, help him. "Look, Ed, Mary's kids think she was in very bad shape when she signed the will. I'd like to learn about your dad's procedures with wills. I need to see whatever notes he may have made, and who paid for the will. I want to know about Hal Morton, the other witness, and where he might be. Any of that information could get Mary's kids a share in their mother's estate. They really need it, and from what I've heard their father doesn't give a damn about them. He'll probably drink up whatever's in the estate. The kids think their father pressured her into signing."

Cohan cleared his throat. "I feel for the kids. I'll do what I can for you. I don't think I'll be much help in finding Hal. He was at my dad's funeral, and I did a little real estate work with him, but I haven't seen or heard from him in years."

"What about the records, especially your dad's billing file?"

"I'll look, but I don't think they're around. Probably destroyed years ago."

"Thanks, Ed. I'd appreciate whatever you can do."

"I'll try."

AT 6:30, AS IAN WAS ABOUT to leave the office for home he saw the phone flashing in the reception area. Since he was the last one in the office, he picked it up. "Rooney and Associates."

"Ian Elkins," boomed a familiar voice.

"Speaking."

"What the hell's happening with my wife's case?"

"That you, Roger?"

"It's Mr. Linden."

Ian put his attaché case down. He was going to be even later for dinner. "I've kept your wife informed, Roger."

"What's this I hear about the motion to remove my brother- in-law being delayed? Who authorized you to give him two more weeks?"

Ian heard a sound that sounded like the tinkle of ice in a glass. The son-of-a-bitch must be home having a drink. "*I* didn't give him two more weeks. The judge did."

"How did you let him do that? I thought you had more influence in that court."

"Judge Anderson makes the decisions in his court, and he calls them as he sees them."

". . .When's it on again?"

"A week from tomorrow."

"What'll happen then?"

"If they file the account and apply for judicial settlement, I assume the case will just move ahead."

"And if they don't?" Roger's voice sounded slightly slurred.

"I've asked that Mr. Kronen be removed and charged with the legals."

"Will the judge do that?"

"I hope so, but I don't have a crystal ball."

"Well, he'd better, or I'll get myself a better lawyer."

"I suggest you discuss that with your wife." Ian hung up before Linden could reply. As he picked up his case, Ian considered how much better his life would be if Barbara Linden were a widow.

"MR. ROONEY WANTS TO SEE YOU now," said the receptionist when Ian returned from court the next day.

"Order me a salad, Rosie," he replied as he leafed through his messages and mail.

"Your salad's on his desk, . . . but be careful. He's—he's in a touchy mood, you'll see."

The big man was behind his desk, sunlight from the far window falling over his left shoulder and illuminating the file he was reading. To his right sat a mug of coffee and two ten-inch paper plates one containing a half-eaten foot-long meatball hero, the other a stack of chocolate covered donuts, the far side of the desk was occupied by Ian's chef's salad, in a rectangular- aluminum container covered with a clear plastic lid, and a container of coffee.

"Hey, Mark, what happened?" Ian asked. "You were doing so well on your diet. You must've lost at least ten pounds."

"Don't bug me today," Rooney growled, pointing to the visitor's chair in front of Ian's lunch.

The latter obeyed, seated himself, opened the salad, and took a sip of coffee.

For the next ten minutes the two ate in frozen silence. Finally Rooney barked, "That *stupid* son of a *bitch*!"

"Who?"

"Who do you think? . . . My fucking brother-in-law."

"What happened?"

"Kathy drove me crazy last night."

"About Barney?"

Rooney nodded.

"What did he do this time?"

"Borrowed more money from those fucking loan sharks."

"How much does he owe this time?"

"Twelve large."

"He borrowed twelve grand?"

Rooney shook his head. "He borrowed ten. The vig made up the rest. He called Kathy yesterday. Says if he doesn't have the money by Thursday, he's in deep shit."

". . .What's she going to do?"

"Wire him the money. What choice does she have?"

"Can't she talk some sense into him? The trust fund can't last forever."

"You met the guy, and you're right. Two or three more dips like this, and the well runs dry."

"What happens then?"

Rooney shrugged, then patted his left pants pocket, where he kept his wallet. "That's not all."

"Huh?"

"Every time there's a contact, he runs the risk of giving away his location."

Ian shook his head. "Anything I can do, Mark?"

"You're doing it now. I needed an ear."

CHAPTER 27

O N Thursday Barney claimed he was sick and left work a little early. He couldn't afford to be late for his meeting with Carmine DiCaprio.

As he turned his rusty blue Civic onto the loan shark's block, he felt embarrassed. While he never could afford a Bentley like DiCaprio's, the Lexus he had driven when he lived in the Bronx hadn't been half bad. More embarrassing were the houses on the block—all four bedrooms or larger, and set on over- sized lots. DiCaprio's white near-mansion was the biggest and made Kathy's house seem like a hovel. He pulled into the circular driveway, was about to park, but had second thoughts and parked in the street.

He approached the front door with trepidation, but when he rang the bell it was opened by a smiling Rocco. "Come on in, Joe. The boss is expecting you."

Rocco ushered him into the office, where he was greeted by DiCaprio. "Come in, my friend. Have a seat."

"Good to see you, Mr. DiCaprio," Barney nervously

replied as he seated himself.

"What's this 'Mr. DiCaprio'? I'm Carmine."

"Carmine," Barney replied, breathing a sigh of relief. He reached into an inside pocket and pulled out an envelope.

"I see you have something for me."

Barney passed over the envelope, which the other put into the left hand desk drawer. "Aren't you going to count it?"

DiCaprio shook his head. "That would be impolite. I know you didn't disappoint me. Come on," he said rising. "Let's have a drink."

He led Barney to a fifteen-foot-square room that adjoined the spacious living room and motioned his guest into a La-Z-Boy. DiCaprio seated himself in a matching brown-leather love seat and motioned to Rocco, who had followed them into the room. "Get us some drinks."

"The usual, Boss?"

DiCaprio nodded.

"What'll you have, Joe?"

"Irish on the rocks, if you have it."

"If we have it." DiCaprio laughed. "Show him."

Rocco took out a bottle of Black Bush, put four cubes into a low glass, and poured in two fingers of the whiskey. Then he poured some brandy into a snifter, served the drinks and left the room.

The two men drank in companionable silence for a while. Then the host spoke up. "Can I give you a piece of friendly advice?"

Barney nodded.

"Borrowing from my group, except for business emergencies, is not a smart idea."

"I know, but—"

DiCaprio held up his hand. "I know. They don't pay you enough at Walmart. Let me see if I can find you a better-paying job."

Barney thanked him effusively and left shortly after their second drink. When he had gone, DiCaprio called Rocco in. "Did you get it?"

"Yeah, boss." He held up a video cassette.

"Make a copy and send it to our friends in the Bronx."

MUCH OF WHAT PEOPLE DO is mandated by tradition. When Ian arrived home on Friday night he knew that his family's tradition required him to be at his in-laws for dinner. It was a pleasant tradition. The Kaplans were lovely people who seemed more like his family than his own. As he opened the apartment door, he wondered what chicken dish he would be eating that evening. "I'm home." he announced.

"Shush, Daddy," ordered Carol. "Mommy's taking a nap."

He followed the sound of her voice into the kitchen where the little girl was working on a jigsaw puzzle. She had completed the edges and was struggling with the interior. He looked at the box cover, which had a picture of a witch's cottage, picked up a piece, and pointed to a spot next to the top right corner. She took it from him, and tried to fit it in, but it didn't work, so she tossed it back into the box.

He looked sheepish and spread his palms. "How long's Mommy been sleeping?"

"A little while. She's not feeling too well. She has a cramp in her tummy."

Ian went into the bedroom where Helen was lying on top of the spread in a modified fetal position with a pillow under her knee. As he was about to leave he heard a sound and saw her eyes open. "Hi."

"Hi," she replied.

"How're you feeling?"

"Got a cramp." She pointed to her abdomen.

"You think?"

"Nah. Too soon."

"Maybe you ought to call the doctor."

She shook her head. "I know what labor feels like."

"Maybe we should stay home tonight."

"Stop being a pain in the ass. Kaplan women are tough, and I don't intend to miss my mother's new chicken dish."

THREE HOURS LATER, THEY HAD just finished dessert and wandered into the living room for coffee and Sam's brandy. "You outdid yourself, Mom," said Ian. "That chicken dish was world class."

"Yes," Betty added. "It was really super. Where'd you get the recipe?"

"From last week's *Times*. It's called South Portuguese chicken stew. It's very easy—I'll make you a copy."

"Hey, squirt, wanna play checkers?" Freddie asked.

Carol was about to say no when Helen turned to her. "Don't turn it down—it may be the best offer you'll ever get from your cousin."

"Oh, alright," the little girl sighed, and the two trooped off to the den.

"My God," said Eric. "I never thought I'd hear that. You think he's growing up?"

Sam took a sip of his brandy, wiped his lips, and belched. "So, Mr. Lawyer, what's new and exciting in your life?"

Ian shook his head. "Nothing you haven't heard before."

"What about your boss's brother-in-law? Anything happening there? I know Mrs. Rooney was very worried."

Ian grimaced inwardly. He wondered how Molly had heard about that. He'd have to ask Helen to be more careful. "It seems to be going a little better."

"I thought he'd been borrowing money from the wrong people," Sam added.

"He was, but that may be a thing of the past."

"Oh?" said Helen.

Ian shrugged. He might as well let the rest out. "Yeah. Mark told me that he'd told his sister last night that he was getting a much better-paying job."

CHAPTER 28

HEY WERE GATHERED AROUND A badly scratched and chipped conference table in a room several doors from the Surrogate's courtroom. It was a Tuesday morning, one of the days when there was no court calendar, frequently used for depositions. The room, small and windowless, not more than ten by fifteen, it had probably been designed as a robing room for the courtroom next door. Edgar Cohan, Jr. was being deposed. Also present were Ian, his co-counsel Tim Kilcullen, Mike Bono, and Sharon Kogen, a shorthand reporter.

"Must seem like old times, Sharon," Bono remarked.

She nodded as she continued to set up her machine.

"How's your dad enjoying his retirement?" Ian asked.

"Happy as a clam," replied the slim, dark-haired woman in her late thirties, dressed in jeans and a red knitted top.

"Her father used to be the official court reporter," Ian told Ed Cohan. "He retired just about the time the courts changed over to tape recorders."

"Yeah—otherwise I could have had his spot." She sighed and finished putting a roll of paper into the machine.

"I wish they hadn't changed. Live reporters did the job much better. You could rely on the transcript," Cohan replied straightening a blue-and-red rep tie that had gotten twisted in his gray-herringbone vest.

"You a trial lawyer, Ed?" Kilcullen asked.

"Insurance defense."

"Ah. No wonder you're dressed like an undertaker. I guess the company doesn't go for real clothes," said Tim pointing to his modified barber pole striped suit.

"I seem to be in good company," Cohan replied pointing to Bono's three-piece brown suit and Ian's natural shoulder blue one.

"I guess we might as well get started," Bono said.

"Won't let us have any fun, Mike?" Ian asked.

"My client'll want to know what took us so long. He's kind of tight with the dollar."

"No sh—kidding," Kilcullen asked, looking at Sharon. She turned to the witness. "Please raise your right hand." She swore him in.

"Okay, who's going to start?" asked Bono.

"I will," Kilcullen replied. "If I miss anything, you can fill it in." He turned to Ian, who shrugged and sat back. He was curious to see the self-proclaimed "best damned trial lawyer" he'd ever meet.

"Mr. Cohan, what is your father's name?"

"Edgar Cohan, Sr."

"Is he still alive?"

"No, he died about eighteen years ago."

"Was he a lawyer?"

"Yes."

"Did he specialize in anything?"

"Mostly real estate."

"But not wills?"

Cohan smiled. "Oh, he did quite a few wills."

Kilcullen had the disputed will marked for identification and showed it to the witness. "Have you ever seen this will before?"

"Not the original, but a court-certified copy."

"Do you recognize any of the signatures?"

Cohan went over the four pages, then pointed. "That's my father's signature."

"You recognize any other ones?"

He stared intently at the page before pointing again. "That looks like Hal Morton's signature."

"But you're not sure?"

Cohan squinted. "Pretty sure. I used to work with Hal, and I've seen quite a few of his signatures. This looks like it."

"But you're not as sure as you are about your father's signature?"

"Not *as* sure, but pretty sure. My father and I were partners during the last three or four years of his life, so I've seen his signature hundreds, maybe thousands of times."

"Were you his partner when this paper was signed?"

"Yes." Cohan scratched his thin aquiline nose.

"Did he discuss it with you?"

"Not that I can recall."

"How soon after this paper was signed did your father die?"

"Less than six months."

"What was the state of his health at that time?"

Cohan exhaled. "Not good. He was terminal. He knew

he was going to die. He had colon cancer—only kept working because it took his mind off the pain."

Tim Kilcullen continued for the next forty minutes but got nothing useful. Then Ian exchanged seats with him. "Mr. Cohan, did you check your father's billing records?"

"I looked for them."

"Find any?"

"A few."

"Anything related to Mary Doyle or Barry Keller?"

"Nope."

"So you have no record of who was billed for, or who paid for this will."

"I'm afraid not."

"Any of your father's billing records kept on a computer?"

"No, my dad was a paper man. Didn't believe in those new- fangled things. I used a computer for my defense billing, but he wouldn't use one."

Since he didn't seem to be getting anywhere on the billing, Ian asked, "How long did you work with Hal Morton?"

"During the time I was together with my father, but not too often."

"How come?"

"Hal was the main salesman at the real estate brokers that my dad worked out of in the Bronx. I would work with him on the real estate when Dad was ill or away on vacation."

"What did you do the rest of the time?"

"My defense work. I really didn't like real estate, and it didn't pay as well."

"Have you seen Morton recently?"

"Nope."

"When was the last time you saw him?"

"At my dad's funeral."

"Any idea where he went?"

"Somewhere in the mid-west, I think. We talked a little at the dinner after the funeral. He said he was fed up with the Bronx and was getting the hell out of there. The pay was lousy and the cost of living too high. I know he grew up out west. I think his family was from Nebraska or maybe Montana."

Ian went on for a few more minutes, but got nothing more.

"That was a fucking waste of time," Kilcullen said as they left the deposition.

"Yeah, but maybe it'll help find Hal Morton."

"HI, ROSIE, WHAT'S UP?" IAN asked as he returned to the office.

She looked up at him but said nothing. He repeated his question before he realized that something was amiss. Her blonde hairpiece was tilted at a rakish angle, her eyes red and tearful, mascara running down her cheeks.

"What's the matter? Are you alright?"

"It's not me," she sobbed.

Suddenly the swinging door to Rooney's wing of the office flew open and the big man rushed through. "I don't know if I'll be back today. I've got to get to her."

"What's going on?" Ian asked.

"Tell you later." Rooney left.

"WHAT'S BOTHERING YOU?" HELEN ASKED after they'd finished dinner and put Carol to bed. They were in the living room, she on the love seat that she preferred and he opposite her on the new recliner that they'd bought.

"You've noticed," he replied, taking a sip of decaf coffee that he still preferred over the organic tea she was drinking.

"How could I not? If you ever took up high-stakes poker, we'd starve."

He nodded.

"Something go wrong at the office?"

"No. . . . Although I learned about it there. It's not really my problem."

She looked at him with a puzzled expression.

"It's Kathy Rooney." He told her about what happened in the office.

"Did Rosie tell you what had happened?"

"Only that Kathy's in the hospital. . . . In a psych ward."

"Is it about her brother?"

"Yeah. Mark called me this afternoon."

"He needs more money to pay the loan sharks?"

He shook his head. "Mark got a call from one of his neighbors. Told him Kathy was hysterical and he should come home."

"Did the neighbor say what happened?"

"She wouldn't. Too embarrassed. When he got home the police were there in the back yard. On a table, next to the kitchen door . . ."

"What was there?"

"Barney's head. Been cut off at the neck."

"Oh, my god!"

"It gets worse."

She wrinkled her brow.

"His penis was stuffed into his mouth."

She hugged herself, and tears came into her eyes.

CHAPTER 29

READY FOR THE MOTION," IAN CALLED out. It was the following Wednesday, the adjourned date of the motion to remove Herb Kronen as executor of his mother's estate.

"Application," responded Harley Goldberg.

"But, Your Honor, after your ruling two weeks ago, there can be no basis for time."

Judge Anderson smiled as he held up his hand. "Patience, Mr. Elkins, we will deal with all of this when I hear the applications.

"Sorry, Your Honor," replied a chagrined Ian. "I should know better." As the lawyers returned to their seats, Ian was tempted to ask what the phony application was about, but he held himself in check. No sense giving the man an opportunity for another snotty remark. He noticed that Goldberg was wearing the same suit. It wasn't in Ian's nature to ask him if it was his only one.

Forty minutes later the application was called. "Well, Mr.

Goldberg, what is it this time?" the judge asked impatiently.

Harley put on his sweetest smile. "Your Honor, I need a very short adjournment. Just a week."

"That's ridiculous, Your Honor. When the case was on two weeks ago—"

The judge cut Ian off with a raised hand, briefly looked down at the file jacket then glared at Goldberg. "What is the status of the account? Have you filed it and moved it for judicial settlement?"

"Not quite yet, Your Honor, but soon."

Judge Anderson was already shaking his head. "Mr. Goldberg, do you remember what I told you two weeks ago?"

"Your Honor wanted the account filed and moved, but—"

"But nothing. I *told* you there would be no further adjournments unless you complied with my direction."

"Your Honor, please hear me out." The man's face was ashen.

The judge folded his arms across his chest. "Well?"

"Your Honor, I finished the papers yesterday and called Mr. Kronen in to sign them, but he was out of town on company business."

"When is he due back?"

"On the weekend."

The judge shook his head. "Adjourned to Monday. If the account isn't in the court file by then, don't waste my time asking for another adjournment."

"Thank you, Your Honor." Goldberg breathed a sigh of relief.

TWENTY MINUTES LATER, THE PHONE rang in a midtown office. "Sally Martinis."

"Harley Goldberg."

"Wiseass."

"How're you doing, Sal?"

"Not bad. To what do I owe the pleasure of this call?" She lit up a cigarette and guessed someone would yell at her for smoking in a smoke-free office.

"Can't a guy just call a friend—especially a lovely lady?"

She laughed. "Cut the bullshit, Harley. You're a lawyer, not a nice human being."

He cackled. "Caught again. You're too smart for me, Sal . . . . Actually I do have a wee bit of an ulterior motive."

"I thought so." She took a drag on the cigarette and inhaled. "Okay, spit it out."

Harley noticed a scuff on his left shoe and wiped it on his right pant leg. "I assume you're seeing our boy this weekend?"

"Of course."

"Where'll you be Saturday morning?"

"My place. Why?"

"Have Herb call me as soon as he gets up."

"Okay. Why?"

"So I'll know he's alive and I can notarize his signature."

"Call him now and notarize it."

"I need it notarized on the weekend." He explained what had just happened in court.

She shook her head. "Cute. What does it do for you?"

"Makes Herb's bitch of a sister pay her lawyer for another court date. Gives her another motive to settle sooner."

"So you think he's charging her on time?"

"I'm sure of it."

"And I guess you're being paid on time also?"

Harley smiled. "*Very* perceptive."

FRIDAY NIGHT THE FAMILY WAS GATHERED once again around Molly and Sam Kaplan's dinner table. Betty, Eric and, Freddie Goldstein, were there along with Helen, Ian, and Carol Elkins, and Carol's soon-to-be-born brother or sister. The dinner, while well presented on fine gold-bordered china and served with quality silver, was not Molly's usual gourmet repast. The main course was plain baked chicken accompanied by frozen spinach and carrots, preceded by a store packaged salad and followed by bakery apple pie and ice cream. "Great dinner, Mom," said Ian as he pushed back his dessert dish.

"Thank you, dear," she replied, "but you know it's not so. I'm sorry everything wasn't up to standard, but Stella is home sick."

"What's the matter?" asked Helen, who had known her mother's cleaning woman from the time she was growing up.

"She's got the flu, and she's not as young as she used to be."

"Please give her my best," said Betty. "I'll send her a card."

"That would be nice," Molly replied.

"Seriously," Ian said, "there's nothing wrong with plain cooking, and I really enjoyed it."

"You really should get a pair of striped pants and join the diplomatic corps," quipped Eric, and turned away to avoid the vicious stares of the others.

When they had settled down in the living room, Sam took a sip of his brandy. "What's happening?"

"Cut it out, Sam," Molly snapped. "This isn't a nightclub, and Ian's not a paid entertainer. He doesn't have to sing for his supper."

"A good thing, too, with *his* singing voice," Helen said.

Sam started to laugh but broke into a fit of coughing as

some of his brandy went down the wrong way. "I didn't mean it like that," he said when he recovered. "His stories are *good*."

"Actually there is something *I* would like to know." said Molly. "How is your boss's wife?"

"Yeah. What's her name?" Sam asked.

"Kathy, Kathy Rooney. She's doing better. She got out of the hospital today, and she's resting at home."

Molly sipped her coffee. "What happened? I hear her brother died."

"He was murdered." Ian filled them in on the details.

"That's awful," said Betty when he'd finished.

"Is there anything we can do?" Molly asked, tears running down her cheeks.

"There's going to be a wake Saturday night, Sunday, and Monday. The funeral's on Tuesday."

"Will she be alright for Saturday night?" Betty asked. "She just got out of the hospital."

"Mark said she'll be okay. She's a tough lady, and he'll be there to support her. I'm going to the wake on Sunday. If anybody wants to go, I'll give them a lift."

"I might join you," said Sam. "Get me the name of the funeral home. I want to send flowers."

"The wake should be a blast," said Eric with gleam in his eyes. "A coffin with just a head and his thing stuffed in his mouth."

That brought more glares. "It'll be *closed* casket," Ian said dryly.

"I'LL SEE IF I CAN GET a baby sitter and go with you," Helen said as they drove home. "I guess we should send flowers."

"I've ordered them."

"Good. . . . Something nice?"

He nodded.

". . .I just can't get over what Eric did."

He shook his head. "Your brother-in-law is an insensitive prick. I don't understand how Betty ever married him."

"I guess because *I* met *you* first."

CHAPTER 30

QUINN'S FUNERAL HOME WAS A block away from Mark and Kathy's church. Barney's casket sat in the center of a thirty-foot wall in a thirty-by-twenty foot room, the largest of the three viewing rooms, surrounded by wreaths and floral displays. As Ian and Helen entered, they noticed a very elderly woman kneeling and praying before the closed coffin, with a line of eight people behind her, waiting to take her place. Ian recognized her as Agnes McCann, the widow of his former boss, Judge Howard McCann. This answered one of Ian's questions. He had wondered whether it was appropriate to pray before a closed coffin. Maybe he'd tell Eric.

Several dozen people were seated on the fifty folding chairs set up in the center of the room, including Rosemary Lennon and the other office secretaries. Kathy and Mark Rooney were circulating around the room, greeting and speaking to people. Mark was his usual hearty self, Kathy pale and strained. "Ian, Helen, thank you for coming." She kissed Ian, and both she and Mark kissed Helen.

"How could we not come? That's what friends are for."

"The flowers you sent were lovely. So were the ones Mr. Kaplan sent. He's your father?"

"Yes. He wanted to be here today, but he came down with a migraine."

"Oh, I'm so sorry—but please thank him for the flowers." She pulled Ian aside. "Thank you so much for what you did for Barney. I thought we could save him. . .but he just wouldn't let us." Tears ran down her cheeks, and he hugged her. When they returned, she took them both by the hand and led them to the casket. "I think you know my Aunt Agnes."

"Of course we know Mrs. McCann."

The old lady had just risen from her prayers and hugged them both. "It's good to see you, Ian . . . and Helen. It's a shame it's not on a happier occasion. The last time was at Howard's wake. He was so, you know, so fond of you."

"We miss him," Ian replied. "He was a super boss and a great friend."

The Rooneys introduced them to several of the other guests, then went off to greet the newer arrivals. Ian and Helen took seats with the office staff. "I like your outfit," he said to Rosie. He'd never seen her in a dark, tailored suit, with her hairpiece on straight.

"It's my funeral outfit. Don't expect to see me in it at the office."

"Not my job," he replied. "I'm not the dress code monitor."

"Gee those roses smell sweet."

He nodded.

They schmoozed for nearly half an hour before Ian

thought it time to make their farewells. Before he could tell Helen, she excused herself to go to the ladies room. When she hadn't returned after fifteen minutes, he began to get concerned. It showed on his face. "Something the matter, Mr. Elkins?" Rosemary Lennon asked.

"Helen's been in the ladies room a long time. I hope she's alright."

"Want me to check?"

"Would you?"

Rosie left and returned five minutes later. "Give me your cell phone."

Ian puzzled, handed it to her.

"Mrs. Elkins wants to call her doctor. She thinks she's in labor."

TWO HOURS LATER HELEN WAS lying in bed in a labor room in Montefiore Hospital. Ian had driven her there straight from the funeral home. He was pacing back and forth in the waiting room while Helen was being examined by her obstetrician. "Sit down already. You're driving us crazy," said Betty, who had driven Molly to the hospital as soon as Ian called them.

"What the hell's taking so long?"

"The doctor's just doing a thorough job," Molly replied.

"Sorry, but the waiting's just driving me out of my mind." He allowed himself to be led to one of the blue plastic-covered chairs.

Molly wrinkled her nose at the odor of stale coffee emanating from a paper cup on the table in front of her seat, then picked it up and dumped it in a garbage container.

"Wonder what it'll be?" Betty remarked. "My nutty sister and her surprises. I never could *stand* not knowing."

"What're you going to name the baby?" Molly asked. "Carol's named after my mother."

"'Jack,' after my dad, if it's a boy. Otherwise, 'Hannah' after Sam's mother. If we'd waited, it could have been 'Linda,' after my mom."

"Sometimes I think the Christians have the right idea, naming a baby after the living," Betty commented.

He nodded and let out a breath. "Yeah, and Mom's as close to being dead as possible while still breathing."

A tall, slim, dark-haired woman in a crisp white lab coat entered the waiting room. "Mr. Elkins?"

"Yes."

"I'm Dr. Heller, Dr. Roth's associate,"

"How's my wife?"

"Helen's fine, and so's the baby. You can visit her now."

"So? When?" Molly asked.

The doctor's expression was pained. "I don't know. Labor's stopped. That's not unusual."

"I know," said Ian, nodding. "It happened with our daughter. What do you plan to do?"

"Sit with it for a while. If she's not back in labor by to-morrow morning, we'll send her home."

"And then what?

"I guess we'll start thinking about inducing. In the mean-time, the nurse will call me if labor starts again."

Let's go up and see her. What room's she in?"

"Room 305—it's right down the hall."

The doctor left, and when they entered Helen's labor room, she was sitting up in bed. Similar to a private hospital room, the accommodation was not quite as comfortable. The bed was considerably larger, in order to accommodate the attached birthing stirrups. There were two rolling carts loaded with supplies, one enveloped in a strong odor of alcohol, and two hard-backed visitor's chairs.

Helen looked up from a paperback she was reading. "Hi. Sorry to drag you here on a fool's errand."

"Don't be silly," Ian said after kissing her. "The important thing is that you and the baby are okay."

"I'm fine, and the doctor told me that Jack, or Hannah, is doing great."

"Which are you hoping for?" asked Betty.

"Either would be great . . . although if she's a girl, I'm not too keen on the name Hannah. Ian and I really prefer Linda, but what can you do with tradition?"

As if on cue, the musical tone of Ian's cell phone sounded. "Yes! . . . Oh, dear!. . . . At least she didn't suffer. Thanks for calling. I—uh—I'll be over in a little while."

"What is it, dear?" Molly asked, noticing his ashen face.

"It was the nursing home. My mother died in her sleep. I-I guess we may get 'Linda,' after all.'"

CHAPTER 31

THE FOLLOWING TUESDAY AFTERNOON, THE Elkins family and their friends gathered in Ian's living room. The graveside funeral had taken place that morning at 11:00 without a hitch. While tradition dictated a Monday funeral, Ian had chosen to wait until Tuesday so his brother, Charlie, could fly in from Berkeley. The Kaplans' rabbi had performed the service, and while he never met the lady, he'd been able to give a moving eulogy about a wonderful wife and mother whose illness had kept her from knowing and caring for her granddaughter.

After lunch at a diner near the cemetery, they settled down in Ian's living room for the traditional mourning. Charlie, deputy-chair of the English department at the university and a world-renowned Chaucer scholar, had been able to get someone to cover his classes for several days; Mark Rooney had insisted Ian take as much time as he needed.

"When's Mom's namesake due to arrive?" Charlie asked as he rose from the wooden mourner's box to avoid the cramp that was building in his left leg.

"Thursday," Helen said, carrying a tray with a carafe of coffee and a stack of foam cups to the four-foot aluminum folding table set up next to the living room window. She smiled at Charlie's puzzled expression. "The doctor has Jack *or* Linda scheduled for Thursday, natural or induced."

"I guess I'm not experienced in that field," Charlie admitted brushing back his curly, formerly mud-gutter mop of blonde hair that was lightening over strands of gray.

"Maybe it's time," she replied with a wicked smile. "My friend and soon-to-be-former co-worker, Sheila, is going back to her mother in California. She's sweet, very pretty . . . and her two sons, from her first marriage, will give you a good start."

"Hey!" he replied with a laugh, "I'm not in *that* much of a hurry."

"Just trying to be helpful. I'm told you older bachelors can get awfully lonely."

"I wouldn't worry about Charlie," said Ian. "From what I remember before he went away to Berkeley, I suspect he has an impressive stable of doting female admirers."

"Ian Elkins, are you trying to say that a normal male would be better off playing the field than having a good wife and children?"

"Did I say that?" he asked, suppressing a laugh.

"You implied it. You men just don't know what's good for you."

"Sweetheart, mother of my nearly two children, I would never say anything against being married to you. It was the best thing that ever happened to me But marriage isn't the be-all and end-all for everyone."

She smiled. "Preserve your freedom if you want to, Charlie, but if you don't at least meet her, you're passing up a good thing."

He shrugged. "Okay, you win. Give me her number."

Helen nodded. "Now, if you gentlemen don't mind, I need a nap. Wake me when you get *very* hungry."

For the next hour, the brothers sat together in moderately, if not completely, comfortable silence. Then Charlie rose again to stretch his legs. "I could do with some coffee. Want some?"

Ian shook his head.

Charlie poured himself one, added milk and sweetener, and returned to his seat. "You know, I'm really not a hundred percent against marriage."

"As long as it's not you."

Charlie chuckled. "It's true. It was nice of Mom and Dad to take the step. Otherwise I could have been a literal bastard."

"Would that have been better than 'literary'?"

Charlie laughed. "Good line. We should make time to trade quips more often. . . . But seriously, I'm not against *my* getting married. I just haven't found the right woman. If I ever run into a clone of Mom . . . or Helen, come to think of it, I could be persuaded to take the step."

"If you found a woman like that, you'd be a fool not to. I must admit I'm a very lucky guy, but believe me, there are plenty of good women around if you give it a chance. I've met Sheila. She's okay, and her two boys are kind of cute."

"I'll see," Charlie replied with a shrug.

"Ian, can you please come into the bedroom!" Helen shouted.

"I get you something, sweetie?"

She shook her head and winced.

"You okay?"

"Considering. Labor's started again. I've been timing it, and they're coming about every eight or nine minutes. I called Dr. Roth, and she told me to come in now. Sorry to break up your *shiva*."

"Hey, first things first. What do you need to take with you?"

"My bag's packed. It's on the floor of my closet."

At eight thirty-five that evening, weighing in at seven pounds eleven ounces, Linda Elkins made her debut.

AT SIX FORTY-FIVE ON WEDNESDAY MORNING, the clock-radio on Sally Martinis' night table went off. She snuggled deeper into the covers and, for the next five minutes, ignored the news on WINS. Then her head exploded, and she reached out and slapped at the set until the buzzer went off. She felt like shit. The menstrual cramps that had begun the prior Saturday had ruined her weekend sex with Herb, and his solicitousness hadn't helped. While the cramps abated by Monday, the depression that came with them had lingered on.

At seven she dragged herself out of bed, tightened the under-sheet, pulled up the duvet, fluffed her two pillows, and trudged into the bathroom. After turning off the near-scalding water, she wrapped her head in a towel and put on a pink terry-cloth robe. Her mood improved when she entered the kitchen and inhaled the aroma of freshly brewed coffee. Herb had suggested that she use the timer on the coffee machine. She poured herself a cup and took a long sip. She took three oranges out of the fridge, squeezed a glass of juice, put a jumbo oat muffin into the toaster oven, and sat down at the table. Maybe she could survive the day.

As she ate, she mulled over the past weekend. Herb'd been *pretty* good company, a lot better than the asshole she'd divorced five years earlier. Of course, Charlie had had a plus side. She'd gotten the apartment as equitable distribution.

It was, in any case, time to take the big step again. Herb had sort of promised to marry her after his mother's estate was settled. It would be . . . kind of nice to be Mrs. Herbert Kronen. He had a future at his company, and there *was* his share in the mother's estate. But how could she get him off the dime?

After breakfast she made up and got into a navy suit with a skirt that came a few inches above the knee. That would sell the client.

As she was leaving the apartment, she decided to call Harley Goldberg as soon as she got to the office. A smart Jewish lawyer should know how to maneuver a Jewish accountant.

CHAPTER 32

EARLY WEDNESDAY AFTERNOON, MIKE BONO was at his desk in the back room of his store-front office on the north side of 161st Street. The room was brightly lit by a florescent ceiling fixture, an absolute necessity in so small and windowless space. Many of the neighborhood lawyers who occupied stores for their offices used the store front for their desks, since it offered both light and visibility for potential clients. Not Mike: Neither criminal, landlord and tenant, nor personal injury practitioner, he was an estates lawyer; the dignity of his calling would not permit him to expose himself in a window, like an Amsterdam prostitute.

Some local lawyers, like Ian Elkins's boss, rented apartments, but that wasn't for Bono either. He would have much preferred a genuine office building, but there were none in the immediate vicinity of the Bronx County Courthouse.

Thinking about Elkins called to mind the Mary Doyle Estate they were together on, one pain in the ass on all sides. The kids were snots, especially the loud-mouthed girl, Angela.

But Mary was her mother, after all. Tim Kilcullen, who represented the two older kids, was a real character—and Ian, God love him, a damned good lawyer but a boy scout. Worst of all was cheap, abusive, nasty sonofabitch, Barry Keller. Bono scratched his chin, trying to think of the man's good points. He'd beaten up his daughter, slashed her tires, refused to give his kids anything more than nuisance value on their mother's estate. Bono thought he'd better check to see if the bastard had gotten out of jail on the tire fiasco. If he *was* out, Elkins and Kilcullen wanted to depose him, and it'd have to be set it up before Keller climbed back into the bottle. When he was sober, the guy had real charm.

He pressed the intercom. "Nora, get me Barry Keller on the line."

"I have Mrs. Keller," she said when she buzzed him back. "He's not home."

"Put her on."

". . . What do you want?"

Bono shook his head. "Hi, Moira."

"Huh?"

"It's Mike Bono."

"I know who you are. I told your secretary Barry's not home. Now what d'you want?"

Maybe she was what had made Keller what he was. He gritted his teeth. "Barry out of jail?"

"He got out Tuesday."

"Will he be home soon?"

"How should I know? I think he's down at Ryan's, lapping up the juice." She picked up a cup from the kitchen table and sipped her coffee, enjoying both it and the discomfiture she was giving her husband's lawyer.

"Think he'll be home soon?"

"Who knows?"

"Look, I need him for Mary's estate."

"That damn whore and her three no-good bastards? I'm glad she's dead. Hope she rots in hell."

"Will you please ask him to call me?" He waited for several seconds and asked again. When there was still no reply, he slammed the phone down. "Damned bitch hung up on me!"

LATER THAT AFTERNOON, THE PHONE rang in a smallish two-lawyer office on Queens Boulevard. It was answered by a thin, dark-haired woman in her fifties, seated before a computer monitor on an otherwise cluttered, scarred secretarial desk. "Kilcullen and McCarthy."

"Sonia?"

"No, Sonia is only here on Tuesdays and Thursdays," she replied, assuming it was one of Sonia's many friends.

"May I speak to Mr. Kilcullen?"

"He's in court. Who's calling?"

"Angela. . .Angela Keller."

"Oh, hello, dear. It's Kate. How are you?"

"Not so good, Aunt Kate." At this Angela's voice caught, as if she was trying to hold back tears. ". . . I'm *scared*."

"What happened?"

"My father—he called me. He must have just gotten out of jail, and he sounded drunk, or crazy. . . or both."

"What'd he say?"

"He started out real quiet. Asked me how I was. I said fine. Then he said: 'Well you won't be fine for long, you god damned fucking cunt. You can't pull that shit on me, so watch your little ass. I'm going to dance at your wake.'"

". . .Have you called the cops?"

"No."

"Why not? He's threatening to *kill* you, dear!"

"I'm afraid to. That might make him madder."

"Why don't you talk to your boyfriend? He's a cop, isn't he?"

"Y-yeah. That's a good idea. I'll talk to him when he gets off."

"Ask him to find out who your father's probation officer is. Maybe *he* can lean on him."

"I'll do that."

"I'll tell Tim about this when he comes in, said Kate. "And I think there's something I can do now."

"What?"

"Who's your father's lawyer?"

"Mike—uh . . . Mike Bono."

"You have his address and phone number?"

". . . I don't think so, but I'm sure Uncle Tim has it."

"That's okay. I'll check the file."

TEN MINUTES LATER, THE PHONE in the Bono office rang. "Mr. Bono, please."

"Who's calling?"

"Katherine McCarthy. I'm a lawyer."

"On what matter?"

"The Doyle Estate."

When Bono came on the line, he said, "Yes, Ms. Mc-Carthy. What's this about?"

"I'm Tim Kilcullen's partner."

"I guess you're calling about the deposition your partner

wanted."

"No, I'm calling about that no-good bastard you represent."

"Hey, you've got no call to insult Mr. Keller."

"Like hell I don't. That prick just threatened to murder my client, his daughter, Angela. You'd better call him off, or we'll see that he rots in jail."

". . .I'll try to reach him." Bono hung up the phone and pressed the intercom.

"Yes, Mr. Bono."

"Nora, get me the phone number of Ryan's Bar and Grill. I think it's on 168th Street."

AT FIVE-FORTY THAT AFTERNOON, SALLY was seated at the bar table furthest away from the free lunch counter at her favorite after work pub on West Forty-seventh Street. She liked that table since the room was less crowded there. Even at that distance, she could smell the garlic-flavored sausage. She had nearly finished her first Manhattan and signaled the bar waitress. Three minutes later the slim redhead in blue vest and tartan miniskirt delivered her drink and a bowl of peanuts.

"May I join you?" asked a tall, slim man when the waitress had departed.

He was quite good looking, and Sally was tempted, but thought better of it. "Sorry, but I'm waiting for a friend."

"I'd be pleased to buy both of you ladies a drink."

"*He's* not a lady,"

"My loss," he replied, spreading his palms, smiled, and headed towards an attractive blonde sitting alone at the bar.

I wonder what's keeping him? she thought glancing at her black Movado. He's usually prompt. She brightened as she saw Harley approaching her table.

"Sorry I'm late—my conference lasted longer than I expected."

"Glad you were able to make it."

He sat down and signaled the waitress.

"That a new suit?" she asked. "Blue pinstripes look good on you."

"Yeah, it was delivered last week. I'm giving it a road test."

"Get some more double-breasteds. That's the style for you."

"Double Jack Daniels on the rocks," he said when the waitress reappeared. "And could I get some pretzels?"

Sally made a deep dent in her drink. "So how's the case going?"

"About the same. Why?"

". . .Just wondering."

The waitress arrived with his bourbon and the pretzels, and Harley took a sip then munched a pretzel. "I needed that. Work makes me hungry. . . . You weren't just wondering, were you?"

She blushed. "No. You're right. I've got a problem."

"About the case?"

"Sort of."

"How?" he asked with a puzzled look.

"I'm not getting any younger."

"Who is?"

She chuckled. "I've been divorced for five years, and . . . ."

"And it's time to get a new husband."

She nodded.

"What about Herb?"

"He promised to marry me when the estate's settled."

He shook his head. "Settling now would be a mistake. It would cost big."

Her face fell.

Harley smiled. "If that's your only problem I've got a better solution—*I'll* marry you."

"What about your wife?"

"The hell with her. I'll divorce the old bag. . . . There is one condition."

"What's that?"

"I'd want a road test first."

She knit her brow, laughed, and punched him playfully on the chin.

"Gotta go now." Harley tossed off his drink, gave her a peck on the lips, and departed.

As she watched his receding form, Sally mused—I wonder if he's really kidding? He's a little too short for me, and he could run to fat, but. . . .

CHAPTER 33

AT NOON THURSDAY, THE DARK-HAIRED, full-figured woman in her late twenties was seated in front of a computer monitor in the secretarial portion of a store-front law office on the north side of 161st Street. The love seat and three chairs in the waiting area were empty, which was not unusual, since Mike Bono's estates and estate planning clients usually came in the afternoon and early evening. She printed and saved the last item of dictation, went to the file room in the back next to her boss's office, retrieved the chicken caesar salad she'd brought from home, poured herself a cup of coffee, and returned to her desk. Nora had to be very careful about what she ate. She didn't want to emulate her mother and two older sisters by turning into another fat Fazio woman, at least not before she landed a husband. She'd gone with Mike right after completing the secretarial course at Catherine Gibbs, been with him for eight years, and quickly become his right arm. Having graduated St. Theresa's with excellent grades, Nora had looked forward to a college education, but her father had quickly disabused her of that ambition. Nice Italian girls became house wives, nuns or at most secretaries. College was for boys like her brother Mario, who had just flunked out of St. John's.

She ate her lunch in an almost leisurely manner, frequently looking at the reproductions that decorated the walls bordering the waiting area. She much preferred the Picasso abstracts on the right side to the devotional pictures that adorned the left wall. She had nearly finished her lunch when the phone rang. "Mr. Bono's office."

"Hi, Nora, it's me. I just finished in court. I'll grab some lunch and be in about one-thirty. Anything happening?"

"Mr. Keller returned your call of yesterday. He sounded very angry."

"I'll call him when I get in."

RYAN'S PUB WAS A SMALL, dingy bar-and-grill at the corner of 168th Street and Jerome Avenue. In years gone by, it had done a thriving business with a substantial Irish American population, but the ethnicity of the neighborhood had changed, and the Hispanics and African Americans who now inhabited the South West Bronx had their own favorite watering holes.

That afternoon, it was occupied by two gray-haired men, the bartender and Barry Keller, his only customer. The former, who owned the place, was called Charley by the customers, most of whom believed him to be Charles Ryan, the founder of the institution. Actually Charley had died in the early fifties and the bar had been sold by the estate to George Papadopoulos, who had assumed Ryan's identity.

"You know what I like about John Powers?" Keller asked, left elbow on the bar as he tossed off his fourth straight Irish of the day.

"What would that be, Barry?"

"It tastes just like Bushmill's, but it's not Protestant whiskey."

"Is that so? And aren't you a font of knowledge." Charley had heard the same question and answer at least a hundred times, but what the hell, the man was a paying customer.

"You know what that wop bastard did to me?" Keller asked, nodding and pointing to his empty glass.

"Who's that?" Charley reached behind him, took a bottle from a shelf, and poured the refill.

"My fucking *lawyer*, that's who."

"No. What'd he do?"

"Ratted on me to my parole officer. Told him I'd threatened my daughter."

"That's pretty shitty. A lawyer's not supposed to do that." Charley grabbed a jar of peanuts from under the bar and refilled the bowl next to Barry.

"Damn straight. . . . I'll fix the bastard."

Charley wondered if that meant he'd beat the guy up. The man had a really bad temper. "Whatcha gonna do?"

"You'll see." Keller put a handful of peanuts in his mouth, crunched, then washed them down with his drink.

A bell rang, and Charley left the bar and picked up the receiver from the pay phone in the corner. "Ryan's Pub. Yeah Barry's here, who's calling. . . . Barry, it's Mike Bono."

Barry took the phone from the bartender. "Hello, Judas, bout time you called me back. What's the matter? You too busy or too scared?"

THE FOLLOWING MONDAY, IAN RETURNED to work, glad shiva was over. He knew that the mourning period was designed to help you get over a loss, his mother had died a long time before. The Linda Elkins he regularly visited in the nursing home had not been the woman who brought him up. The cessation of physical life in her body had been a relief that, but for the accompanying feeling of guilt, would have been an occasion of joy.

After a morning back in L & T court, he returned to the office and received his accustomed welcome, congratulations on his new daughter, and condolences on the death. After lunch with Mark Rooney, he repaired to his room and went through the pile of mail that had built up during his absence—actually less monumental than it could have been, since his motherly secretary, Ellen, and several other attorneys had culled out a large portion of it and dealt with it in his absence.

The most notable item in the remaining collection was a medium-sized envelope from Harley Goldberg with documents in response to his discovery demand in the Kronen Estate compulsory accounting. There appeared to be far fewer documents than he had demanded. This he confirmed on checking the demand against the contents of the envelope. Goldberg had given him half of what he was entitled to. Missing were all of the joint accounts shown in the estate tax return, as well as the powers of attorney that had doubtlessly been used to move Mrs. Kronen's money and securities from individual accounts, which would have been included in her estate, to joint accounts that would go directly to her son when she died. These were the documents he needed in order to confront Herbert Kronen with when he examined him a week from Tuesday. Goldberg was still playing games.

He picked up the phone and dialed the man's number.

"Law office."

"Mr. Goldberg."

"Who's calling?"

"Mr. Elkins."

"What is this about?"

"The Kronen Estate. Mr. Goldberg knows who I am."

"One moment, please."

The one moment took nearly five minutes while Ian sat behind his messy desk, tapping his foot and pounding his fingers on the file. Finally the receptionist came back on. "Mr. Goldberg just left for an appointment. He said he'd call you back as soon as he could."

"Tell Mr. Goldberg that if I don't receive the rest of the documents he owes me by the end of the day, I'll renew my motion to remove his client as executor and charge him with the legals." Ian slammed down the phone. "Bet he's ducking me," he muttered to himself.

Ian had called it precisely right: within ten minutes, Rosie buzzed him on the intercom that Mr. Goldberg was on the line. "Why the hell are you threatening my receptionist, Elkins?"

"I didn't threaten her. As you well know, the threat was for you."

"I sent you everything."

"What about the transfers to the joint accounts and the powers of attorney?"

"You're not entitled to them. They're not part of the probate estate."

"That's because your client stole them from his mother."

"How dare you defame my client?"

"Come off it, Mr. Goldberg. Truth is a defense even if I didn't have an absolute litigation privilege."

At that point Goldberg decided he'd gone too far. He'd told his client that he'd given everything. "Look, Elkins, I'll think it over, but how can I possibly get them to you today?"

"Are you telling me you don't have a fax machine?" Ian smiled as he hung up.

CHAPTER 34

BARRY KELLER'S DEPOSITION WAS SCHEDULED for Friday at 10:30, in the courthouse: The time was critical to Mike Bono. It had to be before Keller started drinking, but not so early that Mike couldn't prep him after most of his hangover had dissipated. As he had anticipated, the preparation was not easy. Nasty when drunk, while he was able to exude charm when sober, the man was firmly convinced that he knew it all.

The preparation went more or less how Mike had anticipated— iffy. He started it out by giving the standard lecture to a deposition witness. "Now, Barry, an hour from now you're going to be deposed under oath. The purpose of the deposition is to give the other side information from you that they can use against you at the trial."

"What kind of bullshit is this? You dragged me here so that my fucking kid's lawyers can ruin the case?"

He was half way out of his chair when Barry barked, "Hold on. You have to be deposed, Otherwise the judge can impose sanctions that could cause you to lose the case. What I'm trying to tell you is, when you're asked a question, just answer it as short as possible. Don't volunteer anything. If they want twenty questions worth, make them ask twenty questions."

"I know how to keep me mouth shut," Keller replied with a shrug.

For the next forty minutes Bono went over the information he expected Ian and Tim Kilcullen to ask, then took his client to the courthouse for the deposition.

THAT EVENING THE WEEKLY CHEZ KAPLAN Friday night chicken dinners resumed. They had been interrupted for several weeks due to the death of Linda Elkins and the birth of her namesake. In honor of the special occasion, Molly got a little fancy and prepared chicken cordon bleu. While the numbers had increased by one, no extra chairs were added to the table, as Linda had chosen to dine at her mother's breast on the recliner in Sam's den. Dessert for the grownups was chocolate cream pie; the two older children were offered ice cream either as an alternative or an add-on.

In the living room, as the adults sipped their coffee; Sam had a taste of his brandy and turned to Ian. "What's new and exciting in the legal field?"

"More frustrating than exciting."

"You won't pay your entertainment tax that easily," Sam, replied shaking his finger.

"Cut that out, Sam!" Molly shouted, jolting the cup in her hand and nearly spilling coffee on her royal-purple silk skirt. "He's just lost his mother, and you want him to be your stand-up comic."

Ian rescued him. "It's okay, Mom, I'll be glad to bring you up to the futile efforts of the legal profession to achieve justice."

"Hey, that's some speech," Eric quipped. "What'd you do, lose a civil rights case in the U.S. Supreme Court?"

Betty glared at her husband. He could be such a mean bastard.

"Not quite that bad," Ian replied. "But in some sense maybe worse.... It's that estate where the woman left everything to the father of her children, but nothing to the kids."

"He was the guy who used to beat her up?" Eric asked.

"That's the one. We took his deposition today, and couldn't get anything helpful. He's either a world class liar, or my co- counsel and I are stupid."

"What happened?" Helen asked, looking worried as she returned to the table.

"Don't worry, honey, I won't get fired."

"So *tell* us already," said Sam, lifting his snifter.

Molly stared daggers at him but held her tongue.

"It started when Tim Kilcullen led off.... That's the older children's lawyer. He's a family friend," Ian added in response to puzzled looks. "Tim hammered at him about the beatings he gave Mary, but the man denied it all. Said he never laid a finger on her. When Tim reminded him of the many times he himself had seen her bruised and bloody, the excuse was that she was sometimes unsteady on her feet and would take flops. When Tim confronted him with the fact that Mary had told him that Keller had caused the bruises, he smiled and said, 'Mary was a shy woman. I guess she was too embarrassed to admit she couldn't hold her liquor.'"

"A real no-goodnik," remarked Sam. "So your Irish co-counsel got nowhere. What did you do?"

"I tried a different tack. I asked him about the will signing. He admitted the will had been signed two weeks after her youngest son, Terry, was born. He didn't remember that she'd had an extremely hard delivery. He said he'd driven her to the real estate office where the will was executed but stayed out of the room when it was signed. I asked him if he knew the lawyer who drew the will, or the real estate salesman who was the other witness, but he said he'd only met them that day, and he denied paying for the will. Then Tim jumped in and asked, 'Why would a woman leave everything to a man she wasn't married to and leave her three children nothing?"

"And what'd he say?" asked Eric with a show of concern.

Ian let out a breath. "That was the kicker. He claimed she owed it to him. The only property she had, outside of a small bank account, was two houses, one where he lived with his wife and legitimate family, and the other where Mary lived with her children. He said the houses were really his, that he'd deeded them to her because of some troublesome debts he had, 'and don't worry about my dear children,' he added. 'I'll take care of them, *if they behave themselves.*'"

"You think the lawyer told him to tell those lies?" Molly asked.

"No, Mom, Mike Bono's a decent, ethical lawyer. He'd never suborn perjury. His client's the liar."

Eric snickered.

AT EIGHT-THIRTY ON SUNDAY MORNING, Herb Kronen was on his back, sleeping soundly. He'd earned his rest, having brought Sally to three screaming climaxes before they fell sleep, but the lady had other ideas. She'd awakened a few minutes before, slipped out of the left side of her queen-sized bed, repaired to the bathroom, where she emptied her bladder, strode around the bed to the right side, pulled the cover back, licked his flaccid member to full erection, dressed it, and climbed aboard. Thirty- five minutes later, she'd given herself two orgasms and Herb one. "Wake up, sleepyhead," she announced, dismounting. "It's time to take me to breakfast. I'm starved."

"No wonder," he replied. "You just won the marathon."

They shared a quick shower, drank some day-old coffee, and headed off to their favorite coffee shop.

AN HOUR LATER, THEY WERE seated at a window booth at Malory's Coffee Shop on Queens Boulevard. Herb had been working on a bowl of oatmeal with skim milk and artificial sweetener, and was into his third cup of coffee. "That's what I needed," said Sally as she push back her second empty plate. The first dish combined a cheese-and-vegetable omelet accompanied by ham, home fries, and toast; the one she'd just finished had two waffles swimming in butter and syrup.

"I don't know how you do it," he replied. "If I ate that much, I'd be four hundred pounds."

She shrugged. "I guess I burn it up. I work and play hard. If I ate like you, I'd starve to death. Must be heredity—my mother eats the same way, and she's slim as a rail. . . . What's the matter with you?"

"Huh?"

"You know very well what I mean. I know you're not a big eater, but this is ridiculous."

"What's ridiculous?"

"That!" She pointed to the bowl of cereal, which he'd just pushed aside nearly half full. "You haven't eaten enough to keep a sparrow singing. What's bothering you?"

He shrugged. "It's nothing."

"*Bullshit.*" She took his hand. "Come on, tell mama."

"It's the damned estate. I've got to testify at a deposition on Tuesday."

"So?"

"They'll ask me all kinds of questions about the joint accounts."

She let out an exasperated breath. He could be such a dope. "You expected that. And you know the answer. Your mother finally got off her high horse and wanted to make up for what she did to you in the will."

"Yeah, but I used the power of attorney to make the transfers."

"Oh, come on, Herb. That's what she wanted you to do."

"But who's going to believe me? Besides, Harley told me I couldn't *testify* at the trial to what she told me. Something about the Dead Man's Statute."

"What'll happen, will happen. Maybe you can convince your sister to settle."

"Not with that damned husband of hers."

Sally scratched her nose. "You know . . . maybe I've got an idea."

CHAPTER 35

ON MONDAY, AT A QUARTER to nine, Nora Fazio pulled the exit cord on the southbound Grand Concourse bus. Another week: Not that she didn't enjoy her job, but the weekend had sucked. It had started out fine. On Friday night her friend Stella had called. Stella's boyfriend Bruno had a friend who needed a date for Saturday night. Was she available? Tony was a nice Italian boy, and it would be a double date. "It just so happens that I am available," she'd replied. She hadn't had a date in nearly three months, and Stella knew it.

The date had begun okay. The guys had picked them up at Stella's home, where Nora was planning to sleep. Tony was tall and slim, with good features, and, but for some facial acne, he wasn't bad looking. They went to Rosetti's, a bar and grill in Yonkers featuring a small dance combo on weekend nights. They drank, danced, and had a snack. Tony was a good dancer, and Nora'd thought she'd held her own. At one-thirty they drove back to Stella's house in Bruno's late model Mercury. When they got there, Stella had invited them in for another drink, coffee, or both. Her parents were away for the weekend, so they wouldn't bother anyone.

It was the first Nora had heard about the absence. Stella and the two boys had another drink; Nora had coffee. They were seated in the living room, with the hi-fi on, when Bruno announced that he had to use the john. "It's upstairs," Stella'd replied. "I'll show you." As she took his hand and led him up the stairs, Tony slid over on the couch and put his arm around Nora. She turned to him. He kissed her hard, pushing his tongue deep into her mouth. After a few minutes of kissing he started exploring her breasts. Not being a prude, she made no protest. Good Catholic girl that she was, it would be as far as she would go, but Tony was strong and had other ideas. When she couldn't drag his hand from inside her panties, she screamed, and the other couple had to leave Stella's bedroom to break up the fight.

"What kind of a fat nun did you get me?" demanded Tony.

"I thought she'd grown up," Stella said in response. "Don't worry," she had continued, noticing the front of Tony's pants. "I won't let your friend suffer. Why don't you go to bed in the room I put your bag in?" she said to Nora, pointing to the door of the guest room, off the kitchen. "Relax and have another drink," she said to Tony, pointing to the bar. "I'll see you in a while." She had taken Bruno's hand and led him back up the stairs.

The next morning, Stella had completely ignored Nora.

The bus stopped at 161st Street, and Nora went a block out of her way to get a container of coffee to hold her 'til she made the office pot. As she crossed the Concourse, she thought about Mike Bono. He was a great boss. Shame she hadn't been on the date with *him*, but he was a married man.

She took her key out of her purse when she got to the office but it wasn't necessary—the door was not locked and the lights were on. "Hello. Is that you, Mr. Bono?"

"Good morning, Nora. How was your weekend?"

"Okay," she replied without enthusiasm. "What are you doing here? I thought you were in court on the Ruiz Estate."

"We adjourned the motion. Larry and I just about have it settled. . . . By the way, I put up the coffee when I got in."

"Thank you."

"But I made up for it." He came to her desk with a micro cassette, a tape log, and three files.

"I guess there's a price for everything," she said with a chuckle. The phone rang. "Mr. Bono's office. . . . Hello, Mr. Cohan. I'll get him for you."

"Hi, Ed. How are you. . . . Really? I'll call the other side and set it up for this week. Thanks so much." Bono pressed the intercom. "Nora, call Mr. Elkins and Mr. Kilcullen. The missing witness, Hal Morton, just surfaced. He'll be in town this week. Try to set up a deposition for Thursday or Friday afternoon."

AT 10:30 THAT MORNING, BARBARA Linden has just finished her weekday chores—made the bed, straightened up the rooms she and Roger had used during the weekend, cleaned up after breakfast, and stacked the dishes and silverware in the dishwasher. She didn't have to do her youngest daughter's room; that was Janie's job. She and Roger believed that children should be given responsibility. Sometimes she thought Roger carried it too far by insisting that their once-a-week cleaning woman strip the bed but leave the fresh sheets and pillow cases on it for Janie to make when she returned from school. She loved Roger who was a good husband, but far too controlling.

She split open a whole-grain English muffin and toasted it, poured herself a cup of coffee, spread diet jam on the muffin, and settled down for her mid-morning snack. She'd breakfasted with Roger and Janie at seven and needed the pickup.

Just as she was about to take her last sip of coffee, the phone rang. She picked up the mobile unit and looked at the caller I.D. readout. It was from a Flame Agency, with a Manhattan number. She had never heard of the name and couldn't place the number, so she let it ring. It was probably a sales pitch, and if it was for real they would leave a message. She waited a few minutes then pressed the talk button and checked the voice mail. It was empty. An hour later the phone rang again. It was from Flame, and again no message. At two in the afternoon she got another call from Flame. This time curiosity got the better of her. She picked up the phone. "Mrs. Linden?"

"Yes, who is this?"

"My name is Sally Martinis. I'm a friend of your brother."

"What's this about?"

"It involves your mother's estate."

"What *about* my mother's estate? I don't think I should be talking to a stranger about it."

"Look, I know you and Herb are fighting over it. I'm trying to make peace."

"Why should you care? It's a family matter, and I don't think it's any of your business. If Herb wants to talk to me, he knows my number."

Sally bit her lip. This wasn't going very well. "Look, Mrs. Linden, it *is* my business. In fact I have a big stake in it." Getting no response, she pressed forward. "Your family harmony is very important to me. I'm looking to become your sister-in-law."

". . .I see what you mean. I would like to talk with you, but I'm not sure what my lawyer or my husband will say."

"I'm not *asking* you to say anything—just hear me out. Let's have a meeting. I can tell you Herb's and my side, and *please* don't let your husband know. From what I understand, he really has it in for Herb."

"I guess that's why you didn't leave a message when you called before,"

"That's right. I see you caught me on caller I.D.."

"Let me think about it. I'll call you in a few days . . . and I promise not to tell Roger."

CHAPTER 36

TUESDAY WAS A BRIGHT, SUNNY day in the Bronx. The light streaming through the windows on the left side of the courtroom created a glare that had to be dealt with by partially closing the blinds. Since there was neither a trial nor a calendar, the deposition of Herb Kronen was held there. Under the new rules, trials, hearings, and most in-court depositions were recorded on tape, but Ian preferred to use a certified court reporter. While a human was costlier than a machine, the accuracy of transcripts was generally better, and getting rulings from the judge on objected-to questions more convenient. Considering the nature of his adversary, Harley Goldberg, the decision was obvious, and he engaged the services of Sharon Kogen, his favorite reporter.

Kronen and the two lawyers were seated at the twenty-foot counsel table; the attractive dark-haired reporter was at her machine a few feet away. After being sworn, the witness gave his name and residence. "Don't take too long, Elkins, I have another matter on at eleven," Goldberg announced.

"It'll take as long as it'll take, Mr. Goldberg," Ian replied.

"What're you, trying to play games, spend a lot of time harassing me and building up a big bill? You can't push *me* around—I'll see the judge."

Ian smiled. "Fine with me, Mr. Goldberg, I'm sure the judge would love to hear from you." He rose and turned to the reporter, who picked up her machine.

"N-no, we'll see him later," Goldberg replied.

"Then I guess we'll start," Ian said, eying his adversary and his client. This time Goldberg was wearing a double-breasted gray suit. Kronen was more conservatively attired in a dark blue pin-striped of the same natural-shoulder cut as Ian's brown glen-plaid. "Mr. Kronen, are you the court-appointed executor of the estate of your mother, Cora Kronen?"

"I am."

"Did you file an estate accounting with the court?"

"I did."

"I show you a document marked as 'Objectant's Exhibit A'. Is the document a true copy of the accounting?" He handed the witness a half-inch thick sheaf of papers.

Kronen put on a pair of horn-rimmed reading glasses, rapidly read through the papers, and looked up. "It is."

"And is the document true and accurate?"

"Of course it is," said Goldberg. "He swore to it."

Ian glared at him. "If you want to testify, Mr. Goldberg, we can swear you in, and I'll question you when I'm finished with Mr. Kronen."

"What kind of crap is this, Elkins?"

"It's of your making. If you'd like to see the judge, you can go in there now."

Goldberg let out a breath. "We can go later."

"Fine, but in the meantime, stop interrupting." He turned back to the witness. "Do you want the question read back to you?"

"No, I remember it. The account is true and accurate."

"Mr. Kronen, I show you a copy of the estate's federal estate tax return that your attorney furnished to me. It's marked 'Objectant's Exhibit B'. Is that the return you filed for the estate?"

Kronen riffled through the papers. "Yes, it is."

"Who prepared it?"

"I did. I'm an accountant." Herb brushed the light brown hair from his eyes.

"Is the 706 return true and accurate?"

Goldberg started to interrupt, but thought better of it.

"It is," Kronen replied.

"I call your attention to Schedule E on the 706. It shows joint accounts from Morgan Stanley, TD Bank, and Chase totaling $2,496,288.00. Were those reported in the accounting?"

The witness nervously scratched the back of his hand. "Well, you see, my mother—"

"Please just answer the question."

Goldberg scowled but held his tongue.

"No, they weren't."

"You know joint property isn't part of the probate estate," Goldberg interjected.

"Counsel," Ian snapped, the *witness* is testifying, not *you*."

"No. Joint accounts aren't part of the probate estate." Herb squeezed his intertwined fingers while Goldberg smiled.

"Who owns those joint accounts now?"

". . .I do. They were joint, with me."

WHEN IAN RETURNED TO THE OFFICE at 1:15, he was told that the boss wanted to see him, and that his salad plate lunch was on Rooney's desk. As he entered the room, the big man was engaged in a vigorous attack on a foot-long Italian hero. "How'd it go, kid?" Rooney asked, wiping his mouth with the back of his hand.

"Not too bad," Ian replied as he took a sip of his coffee. "I have it in black and white that all three joint accounts were created by the son using the power of attorney."

Rooney smiled, took another bite of his sandwich, and washed it down with a mouthful of soda. "When did she sign the power?"

"When she got out of the hospital after her first heart attack." Ian started on his tuna salad plate.

"Who drew it?"

"One of Bill Cohen's associates."

"*Who?* ... Oh, yeah. The old lady's lawyer. The one who did the will."

Ian nodded and took another sip.

Rooney finished chewing and scratched his head. "Did the power authorize the son to make the transfers?"

"As convenience accounts, sure."

"As a gift?"

"I don't *think* so. It permitted gifts in line with her previous practices. I asked him whether his mother had previously made him gifts."

"And?"

"He hemmed and hawed, but he finally admitted that, since his father's death, the only gifts his mother had made to him were on his birthday, and then only in the low hundreds."

Rooney took another large bite and chewed thoughtfully.

"How does he justify claiming the joint accounts as his own?"

"Claims his mother told him that, to the extent he didn't need to use them for her care, they were his."

"How'd that come up?"

"I asked him,'Weren't the joint accounts created as convenience accounts?' He said only partially. Said his mother was feeling guilty about treating him worse than his sister and her children, especially since he'd been taking care of all of her affairs since she had the heart attack. That she told him to move about half of her assets into joint accounts that he could use for her care, and that whatever was left would be his."

"Then how come he used the power to create the accounts? Why didn't she sign?"

Ian finished his last forkful of tuna salad. "I asked him that. He said that he brought her the forms to sign, but that she said she was feeling too weak and told him to use the power. He said he didn't like it but had no choice."

"And all this took place where?"

"In his mother's house."

"Anyone else hear it?"

"That's where he got cute. Says his mother's cleaning woman was in the house, and she might have heard it."

Rooney shook his head. "Smells like bullshit to me."

"Me, too. I guess his wise-ass lawyer fed him the line. I'm going to see if the client knows how to reach the woman. I'd like to get her statement before the other side does."

CHAPTER 37

FRIDAY WAS OVERCAST AND DRIZZLY. The deposition of Hal Morton was scheduled for 2 P.M. in the courthouse This time the courtroom was in use, and they had to settle for the jury room. Since Ian and Mike Bono had a cordial relationship, there was no reason to spend extra on a reporter, and they used one of the court's tape recorders, operated by a friend of Ian named Donald Greene, whose retirement had crept even closer. "You're looking good, Donald."

"Keepin' in shape."

"I envy you. In all the years I've known you, you haven't put on a pound. Look the same as when we first met."

"Not quite." Greene pointed to a pure-white head of hair that had once been black. "My wife plans to dye hers right before we move to Jamaica in January."

"I'm going to miss you."

"I'll miss you guys, too," Greene replied, nodding to Mike Bono, whom he'd also known for many years. "But my wife insists. I guess I'll have to learn to play golf!"

"I envy you," said Bono. "Imagine, being able to play golf all winter. . . . I guess we'd better get started," he concluded, responding to a look from Tim Kilcullen.

Greene turned on the recorder, gave the title and docket number, asked the witness his name and address, and swore him in.

"Do you want to start, Tim, or shall I?"

"You start, Ian. I'll fill in if I think you missed something."

Ian was surprised but guessed that Kilcullen was not fully familiar with will signings.

"Mr. Morton, what is your business or profession?"

The witness smiled and brushed back his curly, salt-and-pepper hair. "I'm a licensed real estate salesman."

"Your license is from the State of Missouri?"

"Yes."

"And where do you practice your profession?"

"In Kansas City—Harry Truman's town."

"Ever worked in New York?"

"Yes. In the Bronx."

"Where in the Bronx?"

"In an office a little off Moshulu Parkway."

"When did you leave there?"

"About five years ago."

Ian showed the will to the witness , who identified all the signatures.

"Did a lawyer supervise the execution of the will?"

"Uh-huh, Edgar Cohan."

"Had you met Mary Doyle before the day she signed the will?"

"I don't think so."

"Had you met Mr. Cohan before?"

"I knew *him* for years. He used to work out of the office. Did wills and a lot of real estate."

"Did you know Barry Keller?"

"Never met him before, but I'd seen him in the office."

". . .How so?"

"He used to meet with Ed Cohan."

"Before or after the will was signed?"

"Before. I never saw him after it was signed."

"Can you describe Mary Doyle?"

Morton knit his brow. "She had stringy black hair. Looked kind of sick or tired. Keller had to help her in an out of the conference room."

"Who was present in the conference room when the will was signed?"

"Me, Ed, and the woman."

"Any one else?"

"Yeah, come to think of it." Morton scratched his nose.

"Who was that?"

"Keller. He helped her into the room—almost *dragged* her. He sat down next to her, and Ed said, 'why don't you wait outside?' He shook his head. Said, 'Mary'll feel more comfortable if I stay.'"

"Did Mr. Cohan say anything else?"

"No. I think he was gonna. Ed never let anyone *else* in during a will signing, but he was feeling kind of sick. You know, he had cancer—died a few months later."

"Mr. Keller say anything else during the will signing?"

"No. . . . But he kept staring at her."

"Did you know she'd had a baby just a few weeks before? A hard delivery?"

"Was *that* what it was about? . . . No, I didn't."

When they left the deposition, Ian and Kilcullen took Mike Bono aside. "I think your client ought to consider upping the ante," Ian suggested.

"*Way* up," Kilcullen added.

WHEN HE GOT BACK TO HIS office, Ian learned that Barbara Linden had returned his Tuesday call. "Hi, Barbara, how's it going?"

"Just fine. Sorry I didn't get back to you sooner, but Roger and I were away for a long weekend visiting our daughter in college, and I didn't pick up my phone messages 'til now."

Ian smiled to himself. He wished he had the time be that cavalier in dealing with calls. "No problem. As you know I deposed your brother on Tuesday, and I wanted to bring you up to date."

"How did it go?"

He filled her in. "What I need from you is the name, address, and phone number of your mother's cleaning woman."

". . .Why would you want that?"

Ian took the last sip of his lunch coffee and dropped the container into the waste basket. "If this case goes to trial, Herb is going to try to prove that your mother approved the gift of the joint accounts to him, but he can't testify to it because of the Dead Man's Statute. It prevents someone who is financially interested from testifying to a conversation with a dead person—but if the cleaning woman heard it, she can testify to what *she* heard."

"Oh. . . . Her name is Erna. . .Erna Fuentes, but she's Puerto Rican, you know, and her English is pretty bad. I may have her address and phone number. I'll look for it."

He was *sure* she had Erna's number, but was hesitant

about giving it to him.

When the call finished, Barbara poured herself a cup of coffee. Money, or her brother? She knew what Roger would say, but she wanted at least to test the waters. She pulled a sheet of paper from a stack on her kitchen counter and dialed the number on it. "Hello, Sally. This is Barbara Linden. . . . I'm fine. how're you? . . . That's good. What I called you about was setting up the meeting we talked about. I think it's a good idea."

CHAPTER 38

A NGELA KELLER WAS SITTING IN the kitchen next to her son's feeding table early Friday evening. She was feeling somewhat down, not looking forward to a lonely evening. Her boyfriend Jim had just made detective, and while she was happy for his advancement and the extra money it gave them, the lack of seniority stuck him with a good many weekend evenings. She certainly couldn't complain about him, though. He was a loving guy, a good father, and would be a great husband after his divorce from Sheila came through. Fortunately, the woman earned a lot more than he did so her alimony and equitable distribution wouldn't ruin their life.

She stuck a spoon into a jar of junior peaches and put it into the baby's mouth. He gobbled it down. Her motherly smile turned to a frown when she smelled a familiar odor. "Jimmy, I hope that's gas. I just changed your damned diaper." The red- headed boy gurgled and opened his mouth. At least he was a good eater, just like his father. She dug the spoon back into the jar.

After Jimmy finished eating, she cleaned him up and put him to bed in his crib. Then she made her own dinner, which she ate while sipping a glass of red jug wine. A second glass put her into a mellow mood. She brewed a cup of cappuccino, took it to the family room, and had settled down in front of the television ready to watch *An Affair To Remember*, her favorite Cary Grant movie, when the phone rang. She picked up the mobile handset and scanned the caller I.D. Her sonofabitch father: She was tempted to ignore it but she thought better of the idea. Anticipating the message he would leave would only ruin the movie. "What the hell to *you* want?" she answered.

"Now is that a nice way to talk to your loving father?" The voice was slurred. He'd had a few.

"My loving *what?*" she nearly screamed.

"Well, I am your father."

"Only because you don't know how to keep your pants zipped up."

"What a terrible thing to say, and here I'm calling you out of the goodness of my heart to make you a gift."

". . .What kind of a gift?"

"I thought you and my grandson could use a little money."

"Jim takes care of his son and me very well."

"You could always use a little more," Barry replied with a chuckle.

"How much more?"

"I want to give you and the boy a thousand dollars each."

"So send us a check."

"That's not friendly. I'll bring it over now. . . . Besides there's a little piece of paper you'll have to sign."

"Talk to my lawyer, and if you dare come over here, I'll call the police."

She was about to call Jim when the phone rang again. It was her brother Barry. "Hi, what's up?"

"Didn't Uncle Timmy call you?"

"No. What is it?"

He filled her in on what he had been told about Hal Morton's deposition.

"That's just great. So that's why the old bastard called."

"What'd he say?"

"He tried to buy me off for two thou."

"You didn't take it, did you?"

She laughed. "I may be his daughter, but I'm not stupid."

THAT TUESDAY BARBARA AND SALLY met for a one o'clock lunch at Hurley's, one of her and Roger's favorite after-work stops when they were first married and lived in Manhattan. Then it had been at its original address at 48th Street and Sixth Avenue nestled into a small building in a corner of Rockefeller Center. She remembered reading a blurb on the menu of how, when the land for the complex was being assembled, the owners of that small building had tried to hold up the Rockefellers for too much money and the big guys'd solved the problem by building around them. Actually this had worked out well for both sides, since the peculiar location endowed the restaurant with considerable charm. The bar did well as a near-round-the-clock watering hole for NBC staff. It'd been run by a genial Swiss and his shy son, a graduate of the Culinary Institute. At that time the food had been good, the drinks generous, and the after-dinner Irish coffee on the house. When the father retired, the restaurant had had to relocate. The new address was in the theater district, and the ambiance had never been the same.

When Barbara showed up a few minutes early, she was warmly greeted by the son, who escorted her to a table on the second floor. I guess he's learned, she thought.

Sally flounced in at one-ten. Barbara was sipping a glass of the house red. Both women were dressed in tailored suits though Sally's skirt came several inches above the knee. Almost immediately the bar waiter brought her a Manhattan. "I can see that Herb's good looks are a family trait," she said after shaking hands.

"As is his good taste," Barbara replied with an appraising look.

"Thank you, Carlos," Sally said as the waiter brought them menus.

"What's good?" Barbara asked. "I haven't been here since they moved."

"It hasn't changed. I used to eat there, too. For dinner I usually have the veal O'Neil or the beer batter shrimp. For lunch, the burgers are the best."

Burgers it was, Sally's with a bun, Barbara's without. They finished with coffee—Sally's the free Irish; Barbara drank the plain that cost.

The two women hit it off exceptionally well. Between mouthfuls there wasn't a moment's silence. The conversation ranged from politics and current events to sports and fashion. The only subject they avoided was the purpose of the meeting.

Finally, when the waiter dropped off the check, Barbara asked, "You wanted to talk about my mother's estate?"

"I did."

"Before you get started, I'd like to say I think we could become great sisters-in-law."

Sally nodded. "You're right. No matter how this turns out, I think I found myself a friend, and I don't have many women friends. It's the estate that's the problem. Herb doesn't think his mother treated him too well."

Barbara laughed. "That's the understatement of the year. She screwed him royally. I think that, except for my father, she hated men. . . . And come to think of it, I'm not so sure how she really felt about Dad. *I* understand why Herb did what he did, but I wish he'd talked to me first."

"If he had, what would you have done?"

Barbara leaned her chin on her fist and shook her head. "I might have been able to work it out with Roger. He's the real problem. Rog is basically a good guy—good husband, good father, and he was good to my mom, but he never really liked Herb. He's tried not to show it, but, you know. . . . I was shocked when I learned what was in Mom's will. I'd always assumed that she'd go fifty-fifty between Herb and me—maybe throw the girls a little extra—but not what she did. If I'd known in advance, I'd have tried to talk her out of it. If Herb had talked to me in advance, said that he needed more, I could have talked to Roger. I know he'd never let me give away any of the girls' money, but he knew what Mom did was unfair. I think he'd at least have gone along with splitting the two-thirds evenly instead of sixty-forty. But since Herb pulled that joint account business, Rog's been calling him a crook and feels justified in hating him."

"So what're you going to do?"

"I wish I knew. You have any ideas?"

"Maybe if you and Herb could sit down alone together—

without husbands, or lawyers . . . yeah, and without me."

Barbara let out a breath. "It's a thought. Let me mull it over. In any event, I'm glad we met."

They departed with a warm hug and a kiss.

CHAPTER 39

AT ONE FORTY-FIVE THE FOLLOWING Tuesday afternoon, Mark Rooney was swallowing diet Coke before biting into the second half of an extra-large steak and onion hero. "Hi, kid," he said as Ian came into the room and sat down in front of the fruit salad and cottage cheese plate. "The judge hold you hostage?"

"It was worth it. I'd just finished the Suarez trial and the judge was telling the landlord not to try again until he had a better case."

"You did great. I told you you'd win it."

Ian rose from his seat, went behind Rooney, readjusted the blinds so that the sun wouldn't shine directly into his eyes as he ate, and returned.

Conversation was suspended for the next fifteen minutes while the two consumed their lunch. "So what did you want to see me about?" Rooney asked after washing down the last bite of his sandwich with the balance of the soda.

"The Kronen estate." Ian took a sip of coffee and wiped

the corner of his mouth with his thumb. "I've got a client problem."

"I thought she liked you. She paying her bills?"

"She's up to date, and we get along fine. That's not the problem. I think she wants me to lose the case."

Rooney knit his brow. "Huh?"

"Remember, last week, I told you about my deposition of the son?"

"You were going to get in touch with the cleaning woman to see if she heard the old lady say he could keep what was left in the joint accounts.... Client know how to reach her?"

"I think so, but she won't tell me."

"That's nuts. Doesn't she know that, if the woman didn't hear anything, we've got a sure winner—probably summary judgment?"

"That's what I told her."

"And?"

Ian chuckled. "You sound like my wife."

Rooney nodded. "Mine, too."

"Anyway, she said she'd look for the address, and when I didn't hear from her, I called again. She told me she didn't want to involve the cleaning woman. When I asked her why, she said she didn't want to discuss it on the phone, but she'd come in. I saw her yesterday afternoon. She told me that she thinks her mother treated her brother terribly, and she wants to try to make up for it."

Rooney shook his head. "So let her make him a gift from her share of the estate."

Ian let out a breath. "That may not be possible. Her husband has no use for his brother-in-law, especially since he pulled that joint account scam. He thinks Herb is a crook and doesn't want her to give him a dime. Before that he probably would have approved her throwing him a bone."

"I remember what you've been telling me about the guy. Maybe we can lean on him to give a little to reduce litigation expenses."

"We've got a problem on the other side, too. She had a meeting with her brother a few days ago. He'd like to make a reasonable settlement, but his lawyer is pressing him to shoot for the moon."

Rooney laughed. "That's the no-good prick you've been dealing with—the motorcycle man?"

"Yeah, Goldberg."

"If he gets lucky and the cleaning woman heard something, he could empty the estate."

"That's what I told her." Ian drummed his thumb nervously on the desk.

"You make any suggestions to her?"

"I told her that at our next conference with the judge we try to get him to force a settlement, but that first we have to know what the cleaning woman can testify to."

"What'd she say?"

"She's thinking it over."

"You'd better write her a cover-our-ass letter."

"No can do," Ian said, shaking his head. "Her husband frequently opens her mail. Any suggestions?"

"Yeah, prepare the letter and show it to me. Then tell her I want to talk to her and ask her to come in. We'll hand it to her."

AFTER LUNCH THAT AFTERNOON, MIKE BONO returned to his office. "Any calls, Nora?"

She averted her eyes as she handed him a fingerful of message slips.

"What's the matter?"

"Nothing."

"Come off it," he replied, noticing her puffy eyes and tear-stained makeup. "You've been crying."

"I don't want to talk about it."

He looked through the message slips. "That's not Mr. Keller's phone number, and . . . it's not your handwriting. You know where he is?"

"Ryan's."

"When did he call?"

"He didn't call." She added in response to his puzzled look, "He was here."

"Did he say or do anything?"

She started to cry again, shook her head, then buried her face in her hands. He squatted down, put an arm around her shoulder, and, when she lifted her face blotted her tears with a tissue. "Go wash your face," he said when the tears abated.

"I'm sorry," she said on returning from the bathroom a few minutes later with a fresh face. "I guess I'm just too sensitive."

". . .What did he say?"

"It's not that I never heard most of those words, but I can't remember anybody ever saying them to *me*. He came in about eleven-thirty and said you wanted to see him. I told him you were in court, and after looking in your appointment book said I didn't see an appointment for him. Then he started screaming curses at me, and shook his fist. I was afraid he'd hit me. He wrote his name and the phone number in your message book said, 'Tell that wop shyster I'm at my office,' and stomped out."

"I'm sorry, Nora. I'll talk to him." He picked up the phone and dialed.

"Ryan's Pub."

"Let me talk to Barry Keller."

"And who shall I say is calling?"

"His lawyer, Ryan. Cut the crap."

"Yes, counselor?" It was Keller's slurred voice.

"What the hell do you mean cursing my secretary out?"

"I cursed no one out. You should fire that snotty bitch. She had the nerve to tell me I had no appointment . . . and come to think of it, where were you?"

"In court, and you had no appointment. I left a message a few days ago for you to see me. That meant that you make an appointment. However, I can see you now, so come over."

"I've been to your office, and you weren't there. Now you can come to *my* office." The line went dead.

Mike had a series of reactions to this. The first was to write the bastard a letter telling him to get another lawyer. That was followed by a bracing realization. The guy did owe him seventy-eight hundred dollars, and it would be easier to collect if he could close out the estate. Maybe he should wander over to the bar . . . but that would forfeit his dignity. If he did it once, Barry would insist on having all of his meetings at Ryan's.

Before he could get to alternative three, the phone rang. It was Charlie Ryan telling him that Barry was on his way.

"Nora, Mr. Keller will be here shortly. I'll be at my desk. Buzz me when he gets here. If he gives you a hard time, buzz me twice."

FIFTEEN MINUTES LATER, BONO WAS seated behind his desk when Keller arrived. The air was instantly suffused with the odor of Irish whiskey. "Well, now I'm here. What the hell do you want?"

"Read this." Bono handed him several pages of his deposition.

"If I wanted to read, I'd go to the library."

"Cut the crap and *read*!" Bono pointed his finger at Keller. "Is it true?" he asked when the man had finished.

"Of course it is."

"Now read this." He gave him a number of pages from Hal Morton's deposition.

"*So*?" Keller barked after he'd done so.

"It's a lot different that what you testified to."

"Are you calling me a liar?"

"No, but a judge and jury might think about it."

". . .So what are you telling me?"

"That you're running a risk of losing the entire estate, and that you should think carefully about making a settlement."

"I offered me daughter a settlement, and she turned me down flat."

"How much did you offer?"

"Two thousand dollars."

"Why didn't you spit in her face?" Bono demanded.

"I couldn't. We were on the phone."

"Well, *six* thousand wouldn't come close to a settlement. It's less than you offered Terry."

"The two thou was only for the bitch. I'd give a little more to the other kids. What do you think I should do?"

Bono smiled. He'd gotten the man's attention. "As I see it, the main assets of the estate are the two houses. One you and your wife, and her kids live in, and the other is where the two boys live. Why don't you give them that house? I'm sure your daughter would agree."

"*What?*" Keller shouted, banging his fist on the desk. "How much are those bastards paying you?"

"Barry, I'm trying to *help* you. You *know* that."

The man sat silently for a moment then exhaled some more Bushmills. "I'll think about it." He rose and left the office.

CHAPTER 40

T HAT WAS SUPER," SAID HERB, pushing aside an empty plate of veal piccata over linguine.

"Why thank you—and I know you meant it."

Sally took a sip of Shiraz.

"How could you tell?"

"It's the first time I've ever seen you finish a dish."

"Too good to leave any."

"I hope you left a *little* room. The dessert's even better."

"What is it?"

"One of your favorites."

"Tiramisu?"

She nodded.

"You are a hell of a talented lady."

"You'd better believe it," she replied, rising to get the dessert out of the refrigerator and bring it to the living room, together with coffee and Sambucca.

A half hour later they were relaxing on the couch. "This was great. What's it about?"

"Huh?"

"Well, here it is a Wednesday evening, and you invite me up for a fabulous dinner, knowing full well that we both have to be at work early tomorrow, so that I'll have to leave pretty soon and we won't be able to finish the evening as it deserves."

"Are you hinting that I might be devious?"

"You could say that."

"And you'd be right. I always have a few ulterior motives."

"How many you say?"

"Two's enough."

He laughed. "Well?"

"In the first place, tonight was a little sample of what it would be like to come home to me every night. . . . And we could go to bed, and still get up in time for work."

He shook his head. "Look, I've told you at least a dozen times, just as soon as I settle my mother's estate, we can get married."

"I know that," she replied, running her fingertips up and down the inside of his thigh. "That's my second ulterior motive."

He knit his brow.

"You had that meeting with Barbara on Monday," she said.

"Yeah. She filled me in on what's holding that up. . . . You two are really getting along."

"She's great. We're going to be like sisters."

"She's big on you, too. . . . What did you come up with?"

"As we see it, there are two people holding up the settlement."

"Right, Roger and Harley. What do we do about them?"

"Roger's the easier one."

He shook his head. "You're out of your mind. He'd never let Barbara settle, and she's afraid to cross him."

"True, but he'll have no choice if the judge jams it down your throats."

"Uh-huh. . . . And Harley?"

"That's obvious. He's being a pig."

"He's only trying to get the most dollars for me. . . . Any way, you've been pushing me to go *along* with him."

"That was before I knew how weak your case was."

His eye twitched. "Who told you that? Barbara?"

"Yes—and don't get defensive. Her lawyer told her that, unless someone *heard* your mother tell you that you could keep the balance of the joint accounts after she died, you'd lose the case, and you testified that the only one who *could* have heard her was the cleaning woman, who doesn't speak English. He said that, once he gets the cleaning woman out of the way, he'll win on summary judgment."

". . . Harley never told *me* that."

"Then you'd better talk to the guy."

"I will, but . . . why doesn't her lawyer do what he said?"

"Because she's holding him back. She wants to help you, . . . and come to think of it, me, too."

THAT SUNDAY THE ELKINSES AND CROWLEYS took their families to the Bronx Zoo. Ian and Herb had been best friends when they worked together for the court, and still thought of each other that way. The problem was that Ian was in private practice while Herb was back as head of the law department in the surrogate's court, so the best their different schedules would allow was an occasional lunch. Their wives were also good friends, but again the schedules didn't mesh. Going out together on a Saturday night was a problem, since babysitters were expensive and the grandparents were not always available to sit. When Alice Crowley called and suggested a Sunday zoo excursion, Helen had jumped at it. Their daughters Sue, and Carol, were the same age, and Linda could go along for the ride. Even the weather cooperated, going from a frigid rainy Saturday to a bright sunny Sunday with temperatures in the fifties.

"Daddy, let's go see the blesbok," said Sue, short and slightly chubby, the spitting image of her mother.

"What's that?" asked Carol.

"It's great. You'll see," Sue replied, pulling her friend along.

The two older girls and their fathers led the way towards the African plains; their mothers and Linda brought up the rear.

"What the hell is a blesbok?" Helen asked.

"A South African antelope."

"So?"

"So my Irish husband has a good yiddishe *kopf*. . . . I think he got it when he married Alice Shapiro." She patted her back.

"What's the blesbok about?"

"The last time we were here, Sue wanted to see the lions and other big cats, but the weather was bad and they weren't on display. So she started screaming 'I wanna see the *lions*!'"

"Typical," Helen replied with a laugh.

Alice nodded. "But then, as we were walking along, Herb had a brainstorm. He saw a sign on the fence for the blesbok and turned on his Irish charm. 'Hey, sweetie,' he said. 'Anybody can see an old lion, but we're going to see the *blesbok*! He picked her up and pointed out into the distance. She saw the little critter and fell in love."

"With the antelope?"

"No, with the name. Now every time we come here, she demands the blesbok."

When the children had gotten their fill of blesbok, it was time to feed little faces, and the entire party turned to a refreshment area where Sue and Carol got ice cream cones, and the grownups, for dietary reasons, settled for coffee. They sat at one of the fifteen tables and chairs drilled into the concrete. Ten of the tables were for four people. Two were set up for six, and the other three for two. The large tables were occupied, so they settled on a four-person table for the women with the two men by themselves.

This breakdown suited Ian quite well, and after a short period of reminiscing he seized the opportunity. "Herb, I've got a problem that could use some help."

"Name it."

"It involves the court, and I don't want to create a conflict for you."

Herb smiled; Ian was his favorite boy scout. "Tell me about it."

Ian filled his friend in on the Kronen Estate situation.

Herb shook his head. "I don't see any conflict, and neither will Bill. This is an opportunity to get rid of a case with not too much work. What you need to get from your client is her settlement range."

"Her what?"

"You know, what's the least she wants to give, and what's the most she's willing to have beaten out of her."

CHAPTER 41

O N MONDAY MORNING, IAN WAS in surrogate's court, answering the calendar on one of his estates. In the front row next to him sat Mike Bono. They chatted before the calendar call was announced, mostly about the continued sunny weather—both reluctant to discuss the estate they were litigating against each other. As it turned out, however, coincidence dictated otherwise. They were in court with routine probate estates. Ian's was number nine on the calendar, Mike's number ten. When Ian's estate was called, he answered for his client, was advised that there would be a decision shortly, which he knew would be granting probate, and was about to depart when the judge stopped him.

"Mr. Elkins."

"Yes, Your Honor."

"I see that both you and Mr. Bono are here this morning. I was about to call for a status conference on the . . ." the judge skimmed a legal pad next to him. "Mary Doyle Estate. We could save some time by having that conference this morning."

"Fine by me, Judge," Mike replied.

"Not everybody's here, Your Honor," Ian pointed out. "Mr. Kilcullen represents the two older children."

The judge shook his head. "I don't think that will be a problem at a status conference. At least, the two of you can start it. When Mr. Bono's call is complete, I want both of you to go down to Mrs. Jones' office and tell her to get the file and hold the conference."

Bono's case took about as long as Ian's, and in less than five minutes the two were knocking at a glass-paneled door on the third floor with the legend *Pamela Jones, Court Attorney and Referee.* "Come in," a voice called out in a low register alto.

They entered a thirty-by-twelve-foot room the front half of which had bookshelves on both sides and a small conference table with six chairs in the center. In the rear half sat a rectangular wooden desk backing on two sparkling-clean windows with the sun beaming over the shoulder of an attractive, slightly chubby, light-skinned black woman in her early thirties. "Well, look who's here," she said, rising to shake hands. "And I haven't even sent out the notices. Could you two be telepathic?"

"Not quite," said Bono. "The judge sent us up."

"I guess he's trying to save you some postage," Ian added.

She reached out to a stack of files on her right, extracted the third one from the bottom, and skimmed a note clipped to the file. "Where's Mr. Kilcullen?"

"I asked the judge the same question, but he said to start without him."

"Oh, well. What do I know?"

Ian laughed.

"What's so funny?" she asked.

"Your window."

"My *window?*"

"I used to have this room when I was in the law department, and those windows were never that clean."

"That's because you're a man. You expect someone else to wash your windows and clean up after you. Don't worry, my husband's the same kind of slob. . . . But back to business. Where do we stand with this case?"

"I'd like to get it to trial," Ian replied. "I don't need any more discovery, but Kilcullen might have other ideas."

"What about you, Mike?"

"I haven't *had* any discovery. I'd like to depose the older son and the daughter. After that, I might want to move for summary judgment."

"What do you say to that, Ian?" she asked.

"He's certainly entitled to the examinations. We can talk to Tim and set them up."

LATE THAT AFTERNOON, IN A much messier law department office, Herb Crowley was busy working on a decision for one of the previous week's cases. Two of his three visitor's chairs were loaded with court files awaiting his attention, the third reluctantly set aside for the derriere of a caller. Most of the desk was also littered with files except for the left-hand corner, reserved for the one he was working on with the papers he was using reposing on a slide-out illuminated by the sunlight emanating from two filthy windows to his left. The room was the principal court attorneys, not for its attractiveness, but for its proximity to the surrogate's chambers. Perhaps its best feature was the coffee maker that Bill Anderson had left when he was elected surrogate and appointed Herb to his former position as head of the law department.

Crowley finished writing and looked over the document, making a few corrections, then clipped it to the cover of the file and added it to the typist pile on the front left of his desk. As he reached for the next file, the phone rang. "Herb Crowley," he answered. ". . .Yes, Judge, I'll be right in." He rose, picked up a stack of completed files, left the office, and turned towards the judge's chambers.

"He's waiting for you," said the pert blonde secretary. "Go right in,"

"Thanks, Penny." Not breaking stride, Crowley traversed the ten-foot long waiting area and entered the judge's chambers through the door at the left rear.

"I'm in the library," called Anderson. The long conference table was surrounded by the shelves of law books that he and his assistants used when the judge was on the bench.

"Got these for you, Judge." Crowley laid eight files on the table and took a seat opposite Anderson.

"I'm done with the last batch," the judge replied, pushing a stack back. "I made some changes on Feldman and Gione."

Herb looked at the changed decisions and nodded.

"The other six are fine. . . . In fact, Reynolds is great."

"Thanks, Judge," Herb replied, glowing with appreciation. "I'll give the files to Penny on my way out."

"How's the campaign coming? Made any appointments?"

"Uncle Frank will be my treasurer. He's a good money raiser, and I'm going to ask Ian to be the manager."

"Good choices. I'm going to miss you, but the civil court

can use another good judge. . . . And, there *is* another plus—
I can get Ian back, with enough money to raise his family."

"That'll be great. Speaking of Ian . . .."

"Shoot!"

Herb filled in the judge on the discussion at the zoo.

"I think you're right, and it'll probably save us work. . . .
That is, unless Goldberg continues to be a pig."

"There's got to be a way of convincing Goldberg's client
that his lawyer's attitude and tactics are on the way to losing
him all of his ill-gotten gains."

"Let's start with a status conference before you."

"I'll add it to my list. What do you want me to do?"

"Press Goldberg. Ask him if his client knows how thin
the ice is. Then set up another conference before me, with the
clients present."

CHAPTER 42

IT WAS LATE ON THURSDAY before Ian could reach Tim Kilcullen. He had called the man several times each day and
left messages on voice mail, but the calls hadn't been returned. Finally he reached Kate McCarthy, and explained
what he wanted. "Sorry, Ian," she said, "but Timmy's in the
middle of a heavy criminal trial in New York Supreme. He
gets all wrapped up in those and doesn't return calls. Last
year he was on trial when our mum lay dying in the hospital,
and he almost didn't make the wake."

"*Wow*, that's dedication to the law."

"No, that's just my crazy brother. . . . But I'll tell you
what. Give me your home number. I'll try to get him to call
you tonight."

AT EIGHT-THIRTY THAT EVENING HELEN, was in the bedroom,
giving Linda her final feeding, while Ian was Carol's room,
reading her a bedtime story. Her room had been temporarily
created out of what had been a dining area adjoining the living

room. Ian had owned and lived in the spacious one-bedroom co-op apartment for several years before he married Helen. The dining area was an el off the living room, and when Carol was born they'd put up temporary plastic-coated panels spring-mounted to the ceiling "I don't like that one, Daddy," Carol complained, "it's boring. Tell me about Belly Lox."

"Huh?"

"You know, Belly Lox and the Bears."

"Isn't that *Goldilocks?*"

"That's not what Grandpa calls it."

"What do you expect from Grandpa? . . . Okay, I'll tell it, but he does a better job."

"I know, specially when he makes the bears football players." She laughed. "But you can tell it your way."

He was about to begin when the phone rang. "Hello?"

"Ian. Tim Kilcullen. Sorry I didn't get back to you sooner. This trial has me going twenty-four seven."

"Yeah, Kate told me. How's it coming along?"

"Not too bad. It's an armed robbery. Fortunately, my guy is very successful at his trade, so the money's good."

"Great. . . . We need to get together. Where do you stand with the trial time-wise?"

"We summed up today. The judge will charge the jury tomorrow morning. I'm just finishing my requests to charge. I don't know how long the jury'll be out. What's up with the estate?"

Ian filled him in on the status conference.

"I don't think I'll want any more discovery, but let me sleep on it. We can't get together to prep my two kids 'til after the jury comes in."

"*We* can't prep your clients unless you want to lose the

attorney client privilege."

"Oh, my *God*! How stupid can I get, and me a trial lawyer. . . . Then why do we have to get together?"

"So *we* can discuss how *you're* going to prep them."

AT SEVEN THE FOLLOWING EVENING, the family again appeared chez Kaplan—two Kaplans, three Goldsteins, and four Elkinses. Ian performed as bartender, making and serving a martini for Sam, a bourbon old fashioned for Eric, white wine for the ladies, Cokes for the two older children, and a Red Label on the rocks for himself. "What's it going to be tonight, Mom?" asked Eric.

"Don't be silly, Uncle Eric," replied Carol. "Grandma always makes chicken."

"But what *kind*?" Betty turned to her mother.

"Tonight is French cuisine. I made *caillettes de Nice*."

"What's that?" asked Freddie, wrinkling his nose.

"You like your grandma's chopped liver?" Molly asked.

"Sure, your chopped liver's great."

"Well, this is chopped liver meatballs."

"Can I have it with spaghetti?" Freddie replied.

"Mom, you must be kidding," said Betty. "I never heard of such a thing."

"Wait a minute." Molly held up a hand. "I'll show you." She went into the kitchen, returned with a book called *The Cuisine of the Sun*, and showed it to Betty, who, with Helen looking over her shoulder, read the recipe.

"Mom, you can't serve that. Does Dad know what's in it?" She passed the book to Sam, who read quickly.

"Are you out of your mind?" he nearly shouted. "It's half chopped chicken liver and half ground pork, and each meatball's wrapped in bacon. . . . Now, I'm not *strictly* kosher, but there are *limits*."

"Don't get excited, Sam. Do you think I'd do that to you? I made a few changes."

"Such as?"

"It's ground chicken, not ground pork."

"What about the bacon?" Eric asked.

"I asked the butcher for kosher bacon, but he said his was made out of vegetables and wouldn't work. He suggested I use pastrami instead."

Molly's dinner of meatballs made out of chopped chicken liver, ground chicken, chopped chicken, spinach and rice, wrapped in kosher pastrami, got rave reviews. At the coffee session that followed, Sam raised his brandy glass "to the world's greatest cook, whom I was lucky enough to marry."

Everybody cheered.

"And now," he continued, pointing to Ian, "for the entertainment."

"Nothing that exciting. Want me to do a soft-shoe routine?"

"Don't you dare," said Helen. "My husband's a very nice man and a good lawyer, but when it comes to dancing he's got two left feet."

"Must take after his father-in-law," Molly added to mild laughter.

"Come to think of it, something happened today that *was* kind of funny." Ian took a sip of coffee. "Remember that estate I told you about where the son set up joint accounts with his mother's money, and he's trying to keep the balance?"

"The no-goodnik!" said Molly.

"What did you expect?" Eric remarked. "He's an accountant."

Sam glared at him.

"Well, as I told you, he claims his mother told him to keep the balance after she died."

"What about the Dead Man's Statute?" Helen asked.

"Spoken like a true paralegal," Ian replied. "He also said that the cleaning woman was in the house when his mother said it, and she might have heard it."

"You see, Dad," Eric remarked. "I told you us account-ants are resourceful,"

Sam frowned. "Did you have your client put you in touch with the woman?"

"I asked her, and she wouldn't."

"Sounds like the accountant gets to keep what he stole," said Eric.

"Not exactly. She told me not to worry, but she wants her brother to get something. The trouble is, her husband doesn't want to give his brother-in-law anything, and the son's lawyer wants him to make a big killing."

"Is that the wise guy who's named after a motorcycle?" asked Sam.

Ian nodded. "My client wants the judge to force a settle-ment so that her husband can't object but her brother doesn't get it all."

"And you want to be sure that, if it comes to a trial, the cleaning woman doesn't show up in court and say she heard the old lady say she could keep the balance." Sam finished his drink, started to get up for a refill, but sat down when he saw Molly's scowl.

"Precisely, and the client's not-to-worry didn't make me feel any better."

"So how're you going to resolve it?" Helen asked.

"That's what happened today. When I got back from court at noon, the client was in the waiting area. There was a woman with her. Sort of scrawny. She looked Hispanic. The client introduced her as her mother's former housekeeper. I asked her some questions, but she didn't understand much. She's from Puerto Rico and speaks practically no English. Then the client translated my questions and her answers. She remembers seeing the son at the mother's home quite often. She used to serve them lunch. She may have heard some conversations, but she didn't understand them because they were in English. The old lady had enough Spanish to give the woman instructions, and she has a little pidgin English."

"You sure your client translated what the woman said correctly?" asked Sam.

"Oh, yeah. Turns out the client taught Spanish in high school for ten years before she had her family."

CHAPTER 43

THE STATUS CONFERENCE WAS HELD ON the following Friday morning. Since the courtroom was available, Herb Crowley, usurped the judge's robing room. As he leaned back in the high- back leather chair with a first- class lumbar support built in, he dreamed of the none-too-distant time when he would have his own robing room, albeit in a less prestigious court. "Shall I call in number six, Your Honor?" Donald Greene asked.

"Your Honor. That sounds good. I'd kiss you if you were a woman."

"What's the matter? You prejudiced against handsome Black men?"

"No, just gay ones. Send them in."

Greene opened the door and announced, "Kronen Estate."

Ian and Harley Goldberg entered the room and were motioned to sit. "Mr. Elkins I know, and you are . . . Mr. Goldberg?"

Harley nodded.

"That's a very attractive suit, Mr. Goldberg. Double breasteds are really coming into style."

"So I've been told. Thank you."

Ian turned to his adversary and noticed he was back to the brown suit.

"So, gentlemen, where do we stand?" Herb swiveled towards Ian.

"The only issue is the joint accounts, and I've had sufficient discovery. I'm ready for trial."

"What about you, Mr. Goldberg?"

"I don't need any discovery, but I think a trial would be counterproductive."

". . .Why's that?"

"It's a family matter—brother against sister. A trial will only waste money and create bad feelings. It should be settled, but this *gentleman* won't talk settlement."

"Not so," Ian replied. "In the beginning, when Mr. Goldberg wanted to settle but wouldn't give me the documents we needed to evaluate the matter, settlement wasn't appropriate. But now that he's gotten off his high horse, given us the documents, and his client has been deposed, I'm not against settlement talks."

"Well, Mr. Goldberg, what do you have in mind?" Herb Crowley asked.

Goldberg smiled. "As I see it, the balance of the joint accounts are my client's. His mother told him they were his. But he's not greedy. We can throw twenty or thirty thousand back into the probate estate."

Ian laughed. "Your generosity overwhelms me. Your client has nothing in writing from his mother about the joint accounts. He opened them with a power of attorney that has no gift-giving provisions, and what his mother *allegedly* told him is inadmissible under 4519. When we go to trial, it will be an open-and-shut case for my client."

"You are aware of section 4519, Mr. Goldberg?"

"Yeah, the Dead Man's Statute. We'll get around it."

"What about you, Mr. Elkins?"

"I'll try to persuade my client to let her brother keep a little of the joint monies."

Goldberg smiled broadly. "If you're that sure of yourself, Elkins, why don't you move for summary judgment?"

"I thought you were an estates litigator."

"I am, and I can smell bullshit a mile away," Goldberg replied with a sneer. "So educate me, mister genius."

Ian smiled. The man had just confirmed that he was mostly bluster. "If you will take the trouble to read the cases, you'll find that, while your client can't testify to what he claims his mother told him at the trial, he *can* use it to oppose a motion for summary judgment."

"He's right, counselor," said Crowley. "It looks to me like you're skating on thin ice. Does your client know how weak his position is?"

"I keep my client informed," Goldberg replied with a near snarl.

Crowley shook his head. "I'm not so sure. I'm going to recommend to the judge that he hold a conference on this case with clients present. When you gentlemen leave, ask the court officer to send in the next conference."

Goldberg left the robing room mumbling to himself.

THE DEPOSITIONS OF THE OLDER Keller children was held in the jury room on the following Tuesday morning. Mike Bono decided to use the recording machine. He knew Ian would be a gentleman, believed Kilcullen would behave himself, and most importantly, Barry was into him for a bundle and he didn't want to lay out any more money on the case than he had to. Barry had decided, regrettably, to attend the event, so he could "see the lying bitch being torn to pieces."

The recorder was plugged in at the head of the conference table. It was operated by Donald Greene, who sat with his back to the windows. Since it was a bright sunny day, the blinds were drawn to keep the glare out of the participants' eyes. Greene was carrying a 9-mm semi automatic on his hip. Ian wondered if he'd ever had to use it.

Barry Keller, seated at the side of the table to the immediate right of the recorder, was the first witness. Kilcullen sat to his immediate right, with Angela to Tim's right and Ian next to her. Mike was on the other side of the table immediately opposite the witness, with his client on his left. Though it was ten in the morning, the odor of Irish whiskey wafted over to the witness side of the table.

Barry testified that he had been eight when his brother was born. He had very little, if any, recollection of what had happened on the day of the will signing. He remembered that his mother was very weak after Terry was born, and that Angela had taken care of him and his baby brother immediately before and after the birth. After Mike finished, Tim Kilcullen moved to the other side of the table and took over the questioning.

"Now, Barry, who was with you when your father and mother went out to the lawyer's office to sign the will?"

"It must have been Angela."

"Do you remember if your father hit your mother on that

day?"

"No, but he used to beat her a lot."

"Did any of the beatings take place shortly after your brother, Terry, was born?"

"Oh, sure. He'd come in drunk and beat us all up."

"Mr. Bono," Ian interrupted. "Please instruct your client not to threaten the witness."

"I did no such thing."

"Let the record show that Mr. Barry Keller, Sr. was mouthing 'I'll get you, you lying bastard.'"

"Off the record," said Bono. Turning to his client, he said, "Cool it, Barry." The man snorted.

Angela's testimony was more vivid. She was thirteen at the time of Terry's birth, and she remembered considerably more than her brother. She detailed the beatings her father gave her mother, her, and her brother Barry, but she could not tie any of them to the precise date of the will. With his final questions, Mike Bono tried to close the door on the issue of undue influence.

"Am I clear, Ms. Keller, that the first time your mother left the house after delivering Terry was about two weeks after she got back from the hospital?"

"Yes, sir."

"And at that time she went out with your father?"

"Yes."

"Did you know the purpose of that trip?"

"Not exactly. I think it was some kind of business."

"Did your father hit your mother on that occasion?"

"No."

"No further questions."

"I have just a few," said Tim Kilcullen as he returned to

the other side of the table.

"Now tell me, Angela, can you remember any conversations between your father and mother on that first day when she left the house?"

"A few."

"And was that before they went out or after they came back?"

"I didn't hear anything when they got back. I was busy changing Terry."

"Please tell me what you heard."

"I was near the door when they were ready to leave. My father was yelling at Mom for taking too much time. He wanted her to get into her coat."

"Did he help her on with her coat?"

"He never did that."

"And was there a conversation at that time?"

"Yes."

"And what was said?"

"He yelled at her to 'hurry her ass'."

"Did she respond?

"Yes. She said, 'I'm not feeling well, Barry. Do we have to go?'"

"How did your father respond?"

"'You're damn right you have to go. You have some important papers to sign, so cut the crap and let's go.'"

"You fucking lying bitch, I'll kill you!"

Barry Keller had risen and was about to go around the table when Donald Greene drew and cocked his pistol. "Sit back down, mister, or I *will* shoot you."

The man complied.

CHAPTER 44

L ATE ON A BRIGHT SUNDAY morning, Herb and Sally were shown to an interior booth in the main dining room at Harbor House, an Irish pub in Piermont, New York. They'd been offered a choice of several empty windowed tables on the left with excellent views of the picturesque main business street, but to them, a booth spelled comfort.

A slim, dark-haired hostess handed them menus and signaled to one of the two servers, who took their drink orders. By the time the curly-haired waitress brought Herb his house white and Sally her red, they were ready to order. As usual Sally ordered the lioness's share; mussels *fra diavolo* with a basket of warm bread, and an authentic Irish shepherd's pie that she consumed with a second glass of the house red. Herb had an excellent spinach salad with grilled chicken, which she helped him finish. With their coffee she devoured a substantial portion of fried cheese cake with vanilla ice cream, except for a forkful that she persuaded Herb to try.

As they were finishing their coffee, she tapped him on the knee and whispered, "Look at the man at the window table behind you."

He saw a middle-aged fellow drawing on the paper table-cloth with a black pencil. He was facing Sally.

"I think he's sketching me."

"Who could blame him?"

She smiled.

"Your secretary was right—this place is very nice. The food's super."

"How could you tell?" she asked with a smile. "A salad's a salad."

"I absorbed yours by osmosis. . . . So what's next on the agenda?"

"Jill recommended the town because there are some interesting art galleries."

They picked up Herb's Pontiac from the restaurant lot and drove two blocks to a waterfront complex of shops and restaurants associated with several hundred condominium town houses. The commercial establishments were laid out in an el. The short arm had three open art galleries, one closed, and a restaurant. Each of the shops and restaurants on the long arm had an entrance on both sides. On one side of those shops was parking, on the other an attractive park decorated with a huge fly wheel that had been abandoned by a former factory.

Sally's secretary had recommended two galleries, each run by an artist's cooperative. One was named after the fly wheel in the park. The other bore the name *Fine Arts Gallery*. Each was running a show for several of their members, and each had tables of finger food that Sally munched on and Herb avoided. The show at *Fly Wheel* had some large stone sculptures and paintings and prints by several artists. The sculpture in *Fine Arts* was a collection of metal animals made from hardware and sheet-metal, the featured works by a local New Jersey artist, consisting of landscapes done in water media and collage that Herb and Sally found quite attractive. They purchased several exquisite note cards with hand-painted and collaged inserts that were selling at a phenomenally low price.

Driving back to Queens, Sally asked, "What's new on the estate?"

"Wish I knew. Harley told me there's a conference with the judge on Friday, and that my sister and I have to attend."

"What's it about?"

"Damned if I know. He said something about the judge wanting me to settle cheap, but that he wouldn't let me. He also said something about the judge believing Harley wasn't telling me everything. . . . Wouldn't surprise me if that was true."

"Why don't you ask Barbara about it?"

"I mentioned that to Harley, and he got all out of joint. Told me not to talk to her."

Sally chuckled. "Doesn't mean *I* can't."

He smiled.

AFTER COURT ON MONDAY, IAN came to a decision: The Doyle Estate was taking too long. It had to be moved along. He knew that Barry Keller would not make anything near a fair settlement unless there was a gun to his head in the form of a jury. He had to find out whether Mike Bono was about to move the case for trial, or he and Tim Kilcullen would have to. The first step was to check with Tim, who hadn't told him whether he wanted any further discovery. He called Kilcullen; as usual, Tim was in court but would call him back. As Ian expected, there was no return call, and by Wednesday afternoon he called again. This time he was more fortunate and reached the man's partner.

"Hi, Kate. How're you doing."

"Just fine. And you?"

"Can't complain. Besides, who'd listen?"

I assume you're following up on your call to my brother."

"You got it. I was trying to find out if he wanted any more discovery before I start forcing a trial."

"I'll check and let you know."

A half hour later she called back. "My brother sends his apologies. He doesn't need any more discovery, so go ahead and force the issue."

Ian cleared some room on his crowded desk, pulled the Doyle Estate file, and dialed Mike Bono's number. He was in.

"I assume this isn't a completely social call," he said after the formalities. "What's up with our estate?"

Ian chuckled. "You're very perceptive. Where do we stand? I've spoken to Tim Kilcullen, and we don't need any more discovery."

"Neither do I. What do you have in mind?"

"Either settle or try it. Any offers I can take back?"

"I can ask Barry, but I doubt if I'll get anything sensible unless he has a gun to his head."

"I guess the place to talk about settlement is at the pretrial conference. Are you going to put it on for trial, or must I?"

"I guess I should, but the thought of laying out more money for that cheap bastard turns my stomach . . . and that includes the lousy $45.00 for a note of issue."

Ian scratched his head. "Tell you what. If I don't get papers from you within a week, I'll start the ball rolling."

CHAPTER 45

THAT WEDNESDAY BARBARA GOT HOME at five, grungy and a little tired, but happy. It had been the first meeting of an oil- painting class at the county community college. The instructor was teaching color theory, and it seemed that there was more paint on her hair, skin, and clothing than on the canvas paper she'd been using. She'd tried to clean up with an odorless turpentine substitute, but she was still filthy. She'd always wanted to be an artist, and now that her two older girls were in college and the younger one getting ready to go, she had the time to give it a shot. She would have liked to take a nap, but by the time she got up Roger would be getting home. He liked her neat and clean, so it was off to the shower.

When he appeared at seven, she had achieved her purpose— was squeaky clean and dressed in a fashionable aquamarine slack ensemble. He gave her a brief kiss, fixed himself a Black Label with water, freshened her chardonnay, and sat down next to her on the love seat. For a while they sipped their drinks and listened to classical FM. "How was your first class?" he asked, returning from the bar with a refill.

"Very good."

"Ready to compete with the ghost of Picasso?"

"Not until after the *third* class."

"You're too modest."

They both laughed.

"What's she teaching you?"

"What makes you think it's *she*?"

"You accusing me of being sexist?"

"Yes. What makes you assume that an art teacher must be a woman?"

"Because most of them are. . . . What's this teacher's name?"

She blushed. "Joan."

He hugged her. "What did *Joan* teach you?"

"It was all about colors and values."

"Didn't you learn about colors in kindergarten?"

"Not like this. We learned about primary colors and complementary colors, and she had us make a color wheel—

I'll show you." She picked up a folder from the cocktail table and removed a sheet of paper. On it was a circle divided into six segments, each in a different color. "These are the primary colors—red, yellow, and blue. By mixing them you can make any other. Opposite each primary color is a complementary color—orange, violet, and green. Each is surrounded by the two primary colors that must be mixed to make it. Red and yellow make orange, blue and yellow make green, and red and blue make violet. By using a color wheel, we learn to deal with colors."

"That's great," he drawled.

Barbara gritted her teeth. Roger was a dreadful chauvinist, she knew, and she a bright, well-treated servant. She kept *his* house, cared for *his* children, and entertained *his* friends, coworkers, and customers. He might consider her a junior partner but hardly his equal.

"Hey, I have something great for you."

She looked up.

"You've always wanted to go to Seattle."

She nodded.

"Well, I've got to be there on Friday to close a deal. Why don't you come along, and we can turn it into a long weekend?"

Her face fell. "Gee, Rog, I'd like to, but I have to be in court on Mom's estate."

"What for?"

"There's a conference."

"That's for lawyers. Why do you have to be there?"

"The judge wants all the parties present."

"I'll send one of the guys from the legal department."

"Don't. I *have* a lawyer, and he's doing fine."

He spread his palms.

As she went into the kitchen to prepare dinner, she felt relieved.

FRIDAY WAS A COLD, RAINY DAY. Herb Kronen met his lawyer at the 161st Street entrance to the courthouse at a quarter to nine. Both men were drenched. The waterproofing on Harley's raincoat had worn off, Herb's umbrella had broken, and the rain was being blown sideways so that the overhang was doing them little good. "The building won't open for another fifteen minutes," said Harley. "Let's get out of this and grab a cup of coffee, There's a place about a block away."

"Suits me. We've got to talk."

The coffee shop was actually a McDonald's on the other side of the street two blocks away.

"So what do you want to talk about?" Harley asked as the sipped their coffee and he munched on a sweet bun.

"I want to settle this today."

"Fine, if your sister will open her purse strings wide enough."

"That's crap. You know we have no case. Barbara will try to be fair, but she has Roger looking over her shoulder."

"Herb, believe me, I've been through this. We've got to hang tough or you'll end up with nothing more than nuisance value." Herb was about to respond when Harley shushed him. "Don't worry, we'll talk about it later. We have to get back or we'll be late to court." The two headed out into the rain.

"WELL, LADY AND GENTLEMEN, I see that everybody is here," said Judge Anderson as he looked down from his bench at the parties and lawyers assembled before him. "If I'd known the weather was going to be this bad, I'd have picked a different date."

As if on cue, both lawyers chuckled.

The judge smiled, looked down at a memo, then looked up again and surveyed the four people. "My court attorney tells me that discovery is complete and everybody is ready for trial."

Both lawyers nodded.

"He also tells me that both you lawyers are taking very strong positions, and that you're making the chances of a fair settlement near impossible."

Ian was about to respond but stopped when Barbara kicked his foot.

"Now, from what I understand, the dispute involves several joint accounts that Mr. Kronen created by use of a power of attorney from his mother, and which he now claims are his by virtue of survivorship."

"That's what his mother wanted," said Harley.

The judge glared down at the lawyer. "The daughter, Mrs. . . ." The judge looked down at his notes. "Mrs. Linden contends that the power of attorney didn't authorize the son to make a gift to himself, and that the joint accounts should be part of the estate, and divided in accordance with the will."

Barbara nodded. "Yes."

The judge then turned towards Herb Kronen. "Now, Mr. Kronen, I understand that you contend that your mother authorized you to open the joint accounts and told you that whatever was left after she died was yours?"

"That's right, Judge," replied a smiling Harley Goldberg.

"*Counselor*," the judge barked, "that was a question for your *client*, not for you. I want an answer from him. You will speak only when I tell you. Do you understand?"

The lawyer shrugged.

"I asked you if you understood."

"Yes, Judge. What about him?" He pointed to Ian.

"That admonition applies to both counsel. I want to hear only from your clients. Do you understand, Mr. Elkins?"

"Yes, Your Honor." Ian suppressed a smile. It was going just as Barbara wanted.

"Now, Mr. Kronen," the judge continued, turning back to

him, "was what I said a correct statement of your position?"

"It is."

"And how did she give you that authority?"

"She told him—"

"Mr. Goldberg, when it is your time to speak, I will advise you!"

Goldberg's face reddened.

"My mother told me."

"Was anyone else present when your mother told you?"

"There was the cleaning woman."

"And there was someone else there," Goldberg added.

"*Mr. Goldberg*, what did I *tell* you?" the judge nearly shouted.

"There was someone else," Herb added weakly.

"Who was that?" the judge asked.

"I don't remember the name, but I think I have it written down somewhere."

"You'd better find it soon. I won't allow surprise witnesses at my trials. I trust you will keep that in mind, Mr. Goldberg."

Goldberg nodded.

"I didn't hear you, Mr. Goldberg."

"Yes, Judge."

"Mr. Kronen, what's the size of the gross estate, including the joint accounts?

"Six million."

"And how much are the joint accounts?"

"About two million five."

"That's nearly *half* the gross estate." The judge turned to the court officer. "Mr. Greene."

"Yes, Your Honor."

"I have a calculator in the left hand drawer of my desk in the robing room. Please get it for me."

Donald Greene rose ponderously from his desk on the judge's right, went into the robing room, and returned a minute later with the instrument.

For the next five minutes the judge punched numbers, made notations on a legal pad, then looked up. "Mr. Kronen, according to my calculations, your mother's will gives you a little under twenty-seven percent of the gross estate. She died a little less than a year later, and, with the help of the joint accounts that you claim she gave you, you're looking to get over fifty-seven percent. Her granddaughters, your nieces, whom your mother obviously cared for greatly, dropped from one-third to under twenty percent. That's an awfully big change of heart to swallow. Have you any explanation?"

The man's complexion seemed to have lost most of its color as he croaked, "I—I guess my mother finally realized that she'd treated me badly and wanted to make it up. . . . Especially since I'd been taking care of all her affairs."

"That's something that's been bothering me," said the judge. "When you act under a power of attorney, you're a fiduciary, and I'm not so sure you're acting like one."

The judge turned toward Barbara. "Mrs. Linden, do you realize that, if your brother comes up with the witness to what he claims your mother said I may find for him, in which event both your share and your daughter's share of the estate will be substantially reduced?"

"Yes, Judge, my lawyer explained that to me."

"And don't you think that it would make sense for you to settle with your brother?"

"Definitely. My mother treated Herb badly. I'd like to

make it up to him—but not out of my daughters' share."

The judge smiled and turned to Herb. "Mr. Kronen, if you don't satisfy me with an outside witness that your mother wanted you to have the balance of the joint accounts, I will have to find against you. If that happens, not only will you lose the joint accounts, you may lose your commissions and be charged both for the estate's legals and for your sister's legals." The judge noticed that Herb was smiling. "Is there anything that I said that's funny?"

"It's just the commissions, Judge. It's too late for you to take them away from me. My mother beat you to it."

The judge cleared his throat. "In any event, I think that both of you people should settle this dispute and avoid the risks I pointed out to you."

"Judge, my client is more than willing to make a reasonable settlement, but his sister won't give an inch."

"Mr. Goldberg, are you hard of hearing? I have already told you that, when I want to hear from you, I would tell you. Now I want to hear from your client and his sister only." The lawyer bristled but held his peace, and the judge turned to Barbara. "Now Mrs. Linden, are you willing to make a reasonable settlement?"

"I always have been. As I've said, my mother treated Herb badly, and I'd like to make up for it."

"Do you have anything specific in mind?"

Ian whispered into her ear. "I'd be very interested in hearing Your Honor's suggestions," she replied.

The judge smiled at Ian. "I like your attitude, Mrs. Linden. Now, Mr. Kronen," he continued, "do you have anything to put on the table or would you also like to hear my suggestion?"

"My client wants to be generous to his sister and her family. He is willing to transfer $100,000.00 from the joint accounts to the estate," Harley replied, smiling broadly.

"Mr. Goldberg, that question was asked of Mr. Kronen. You are to stop interrupting until I instruct you to say something. Now, Mr. Kronen, what do you have to say?"

Herb was about to speak when his lawyer turned to his ear and said in a stage whisper, "Shut up, Herb. I'll do the talking." Goldberg looked up and addressed the judge. "If we have to maybe we can come up a little—say another fifty making it $150,000.00"

The judge's face reddened. "This conference is over. Mr. Elkins, I want this matter placed on the trial calendar as quickly as you can."

"Yes, Your Honor."

"Mr. Goldberg, you have sabotaged all settlement efforts. I hope you know what you're doing, and if you don't, I hope you have very substantial limits on your professional liability insurance."

As the group left the courtroom, Herb Kronen tapped his sister on the shoulder. "Barbara, can we go out for some coffee? Just the two of us."

She nodded.

CHAPTER 46

TWO FRIDAYS LATER, THE KAPLAN clan was seated in the living room, sipping coffee as they again digested Molly's chicken *cordon bleu*. Sam put down his brandy snifter and was about to ask Ian the usual question when Helen, "Not tonight, Dad."

"Is anything the matter with Ian?" Molly asked.

"Yeah, he's been awfully quiet," Sam added.

"I don't really know," Helen answered. "I think he's in shock. I've asked him what the matter was, and he kept mumbling 'Let me sort it out first.' When he came home this afternoon, he polished off two scotches, and he's had two more here. I'm driving home."

"I think you'd better," Ian chimed in. "And it's okay, Dad. I think I'm ready to pay the entertainment tax."

"You really don't have to, dear," said Molly with a worried look on her face.

"It's okay, Mom. Talking about it is probably what I need to do. I was in surrogate's court today on two cases. They're the two I've been telling you about. The one where the mother left everything to her children's father and nothing to her children, and the other where the son stole nearly half of his mother's estate.

"That's the one with the Jewish motorcycle man," Sam said.

"He's the one."

"What happened?" asked Eric. "You lose them both?"

"I'm glad you're not my cheerleader," Ian replied with his first smile of the evening. "It wasn't that bad. Both cases were on for pre trial conferences, and the judge was trying to force settlements. The first one on was the will contest, and it really bombed."

"How's that?" Betty asked.

"My friend, Mike Bono, who's the lawyer on the other side, came up with $5,000.00 for each of the two sons, and nothing for the daughter. That was less than he originally offered my kid alone. I pointed that out to the judge, and Mike admitted we were right but that his client had insisted the two sons were trouble makers, and the daughter was worse."

"What happened?" Sam asked.

"The judge blew his stack and set it down for a jury trial this coming Thursday."

"What about the other one?" Helen asked.

"The lawyer came up a little bit. He'd originally offered to put $100,000.00 back into the estate. He raised it to $150,000.00 but wouldn't go a dime more."

"And?" Helen asked.

"And the judge got mad and scheduled a bench trial."

"Bench trial?" asked Eric.

"Trial by the judge without a jury."

"So what's wrong with that?" Eric pressed.

"It's on for this Thursday."

"But that's when you have the jury trial," Helen exclaimed.

"I know. I pointed it out to him, and he said, 'That's right' and called the next case."

Helen scrunched her face. "How're you going to trial on both cases on the same day?"

"That's what's bugging me. I would have asked Mark, but he's away on his first vacation since Barney died."

"You know, *boychick*, I think the judge is doing you a favor."

Ian knit his brow.

"You're worried because you can't try more than one case at a time."

Ian nodded.

"How many cases can the judge try at one time?"

Ian smiled. "Only one."

"What happens to the lawyer on the other side whose case isn't tried first?"

"He sits on his hands."

Sam spread his palms.

JUST AFTER ONE THE FOLLOWING Friday, Ian nearly skipped into Rooney's office. The big man finished chewing a bite of tuna hero and pointed to a chef's salad in an aluminum container set out on his desk in front of his middle visitor's chair. "Hail the conquering hero. Eat and get your strength back."

"I can use it," the young man replied as he dug in.

"So tell me all about it," said Rooney after they had finished eating.

"My father-in-law was right on the money. Putting the two cases on together was the best thing the judge could have done for me."

"Sam's a sage—a lot like Howard, God rest his soul."

"He reminds me of him," said Ian remembering his former mentor.

". . . So?"

"The judge conferenced the Kronen Estate promptly at nine-thirty. When Goldberg wouldn't move from the two hundred thousand, he told them to wait in the courtroom. When Goldberg asked how long that would be, the judge said, 'As long as it takes.' Then he called us in on the Mary Doyle will. 'Can we settle this, Mr. Keller?' he asked. 'My lawyer told you what I would do. Five thousand for each of my sons. I think I'm being most generous.' 'I'm certainly glad you're not my father,' the judge told him. 'I can give you a bench trial right now.'"

"Mike Bono didn't go for that, did he?" Rooney asked.

"He didn't have to decide. Keller insisted on a jury, and the judge sent down for a panel. We picked pretty quickly, and I was able to get a couple of grandmotherly types on."

"That was a good break," Rooney replied with a knowing smile.

"I'm sure Mike would have liked to challenge them, but he'd used up all his peremptories."

"The gods were smiling down on you."

Ian nodded. "We opened to the jury right after lunch, and Mike put on Hal Morton."

"Who?"

"That witness who showed up. On cross I stressed that Keller had insisted on sitting in on the will signing, that

Mary'd looked very weak, and that the father had had prior dealings with Cohan, the lawyer who drew the will and supervised its execution. Mike rested after that. I don't think he wanted to put on his client. By then it was five-thirty, and the judge adjourned the trial to this morning. I wanted to tell you about it then, but you'd gone home by the time I got to the office."

"It doesn't look like you needed my advice. What happened today?"

"First I put in Keller's deposition where he said he wasn't in the room when the will was signed, and that he'd never met Cohan before. Then I put on Angela and her brother Barry. They testified to the beatings. Mike objected strongly that it wasn't relevant and was highly prejudicial, but the judge let it in."

"I think Mike was right," Rooney commented.

"So do I. If it went to verdict and the jury denied probate, I'm sure the Appellate Division would have set it aside, but it worked. The jury, and especially the two old ladies, were looking daggers at Keller."

"He noticed it?"

"Couldn't miss it—and, all of a sudden, he caved in. Mike tried to convince him that he'd win on appeal, but he was too scared that he'd lose it all. So they settled."

"What were the terms?"

"The will was probated. He agreed to transfer the house the two boys were living in to the three children, subject to a $50,000.00 bank mortgage, and that the proceeds of the loan would be split between Keller and the children. He also agreed that all of the estate expenses, including Mike's legals, Tim Kilcullen's legals, and my guardian ad litem's fee, would